KT-393-863

DARKSIDE

Tom Becker

TIMECURSE

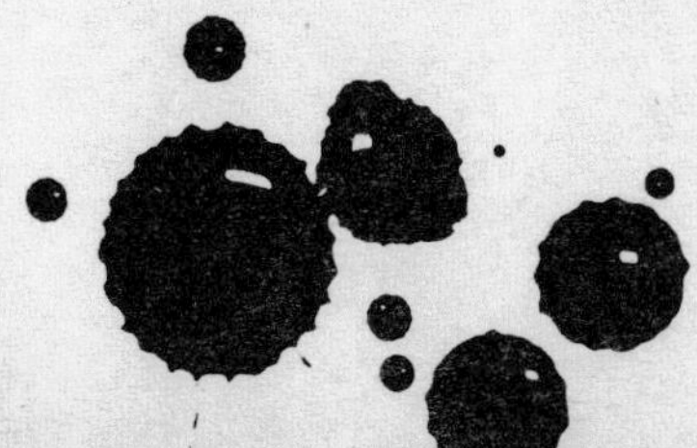

First published in the UK in 2009 by Scholastic Children's Books
An imprint of Scholastic Ltd
Euston House, 24 Eversholt Street
London, NW1 1DB, UK
Registered office: Westfield Road, Southam, Warwickshire, CV47 0RA

ISBN 978 1407 10286 3

A CIP catalogue record for this book is available
from the British Library.

Printed and bound in Great Britain by
CPI Bookmarque, Croydon
Papers used by Scholastic Children's Books are made from
wood grown in sustainable forests.

3 5 7 9 10 8 6 4

www.scholastic.co.uk/zone

Prologue

Dexter Scabble was having a very bad day.

As the clock neared midnight, Dexter, a sinuous weasel of a man with a pencil-thin moustache, could be seen hastening along the Grand, Darkside's main street. Above the coughing chimneys that peppered the skyline, clouds were drifting sullenly across a tar-black sky, and the air was crisp and cold with the promise of a long, deep winter. Typically for the late hour, the pavements were heaving with a surly congress of hustlers and ne'er-do-wells. Usually in such a crowd, the only things Scabble would see were opportunities for profit: deals to be struck, scams to be set up, unwary punters to be conned. But tonight, everywhere he looked, all he could see was the glowering, threatening face of one man: Elias Carnegie.

Scabble's problems had begun innocuously enough, with a tip-off that a stack of crates filled with exotic silks had been left unattended in a warehouse on Devil's Wharf. To Scabble's mind, this was an act of almost criminal negligence. Indeed, it had proved child's play to sneak into the warehouse in the middle of the night, remove the crates, and give them a new home in the cramped back office of Scabble Trading, Inc.

The elegant silks were of the finest quality, and Scabble was hopeful of pocketing a tidy sum from their sale. He was therefore surprised when none of his contacts would touch them – not even Four-Fingered Albert, and he was famed as the least discerning fence in Darkside. The reason for their reluctance soon became clear: the word on the street was that the noblewoman who had ordered the silks had hired the wereman Carnegie to retrieve them for her. With the private detective's reputation for brutal efficiency known across the rotten borough, Scabble was advised to dump the silks into the river and lie low until the heat wore off.

Even now, as he cut across the stream of carriages and hansom cabs that rumbled along the Grand, Scabble knew that the wereman was closing in on him. A lifetime spent hustling had given Scabble a sixth sense where danger was concerned, and the hairs on the back of his neck were standing bolt upright. Convinced that someone was watching him, the thief glanced over his shoulder, half-expecting to see Carnegie's trademark stovepipe hat bobbing up from the crowds.

Further along the street, a handful of passengers were alighting from an omnibus that had drawn up outside Kinski's Theatre of the Macabre. Scabble waited until the horses were pulling away from the pavement, and then, at the last moment, threw himself on to the back of the vehicle. Ignoring the angry protests of the conductor, he tossed the man a coin and scanned the pavement behind him, noting with satisfaction that no one had followed him. As the omnibus weaved in and out of the traffic along the Grand, Scabble maintained a constant vigil. Every passenger was a potential threat, from the urchins sizing up which pockets to pick to the old crones swapping stories of revenge in the seats near the driver. Only when Scabble was sure that Carnegie could be nowhere near did he pull the passenger cord to bring the omnibus to a stop, and step down lightly on to the flagstones.

He found himself on a quieter street towards the south of the borough, where lone passers-by scurried from the safety of one street lamp to another. Devil's Wharf was within walking distance, meaning that Scabble could get back to the office and dispose of the crates before the clock struck one.

He was still congratulating himself on his smart getaway when a pair of strong hands reached out from the gloom of an alleyway, grabbed Scabble by the lapels of his jacket, and pinned him up against the nearest wall. The thief found himself looking into a grizzled face and a pair of dark eyes that burned with a bestial hunger.

"Hello, Dexter," the man growled. He grinned, revealing a row of sharp incisors jammed with scraps of meat.

"Carnegie!" Scabble spluttered, attempting to tip his

bowler hat in a greeting. "What a surprise! How on Darkside did you find me?"

"Followed the smell."

"Right, yes," Scabble replied, silently cursing his stupidity. No wonder he had failed to lose Carnegie – it would have been child's play for the wereman to track his scent. "What can I do for you?"

"This morning I had a visit from a Lady Crystal della Rosa. I'm sure you'll know the name. The poor lady was extremely distressed – it seems a consignment of very expensive silks has disappeared. For some reason, when I thought about things mysteriously vanishing down at Devil's Wharf, your name popped into my head. Now, why do you suppose that might be?"

"Carnegie – I'm hurt!" Scabble said indignantly. "I'm as honest as the day is long!"

"The sun went down hours ago, and I've got better things to do than listen to you lie. Either tell me where you've stashed Lady Crystal's silks, or my good mood is going to evaporate."

"I don't know anything, I swear!"

"I had a feeling you'd say that."

The wereman threw his head back and howled, his claws digging into Scabble's skin. The trader shut his eyes, whimpering with fear, and prepared for the worst. But before a blow could land, there came a sound from high above their heads – the slow, sonorous tolling of a bell.

Scabble cautiously opened one eye, and saw that the

wereman had frozen. There was a look of complete misery on his face.

"I don't believe it!" he growled.

Neither could Scabble. By decree, only one bell was allowed in Darkside, and it had only rung twice before in more than a century. The bell was located in a tower far away over the rooftops towards the west of the borough, at Blackchapel, the sprawling palace that served as the seat of power for the Rippers – the ruling family of Darkside.

"The Blackchapel Bell!" Scabble squeaked with relief.

"Well, obviously. Thomas Ripper must have died."

"And in the nick of time," the trader added quickly. "Bless his dear departed soul."

The wereman released Scabble from his grasp and took a step back. As the bell continued to echo around the surrounding houses, curtains were drawn swiftly across windows, and keys turned firmly in locks. Scabble looked up at the sound of running footsteps to see a hawker haring down the street, wares spilling from the suitcase stashed underneath his arm.

"Looks like everyone's running for cover," Scabble said, with a mock sigh. "I guess it's not so surprising. With the Ripper dead, the Bow Street Runners will be out on the streets. And if they're as mean as I've heard they are, people are best off indoors."

"Their reputation is well earned," Carnegie said meaningfully. "I was here the last time they were about."

"Then you'll know how keen they are to maintain order

while there's no Ripper on the throne. Probably not the best time to be manhandling innocent citizens, then, wouldn't you say?"

Carnegie gave him a baleful look. "You must have been born under a lucky sign, Dexter."

His composure returning, Scabble smoothed down his jacket and casually brushed off some animal hairs. The wereman looked as though he was about to take a swing at the thief, but then thought better of it.

"My, my," Scabble tutted. "Your temper will be your downfall, Elias, mark my words. I'm willing to let this unfortunate incident pass, but next time it'll be my moral duty to have a word with the Runners. I won't be so understanding again."

"Me neither." The wereman grinned suddenly. "The Blood Succession doesn't last for ever. I can wait."

With that final threat, Carnegie patted Scabble on the face with a clawed hand and loped away into the night. The thief puffed out his cheeks. He knew how fortunate he had been. The death of Darkside's ruler heralded the beginning of the Blood Succession – a period when the Ripper's heirs would prepare for a battle to the death, in order to determine who would take up the throne. Until Thomas's successor was crowned, order in the borough was maintained by the Bow Street Runners. Usually confined within Blackchapel, these fearsome creatures only took to the streets in the most severe of emergencies. With the Runners looking unfavourably upon such everyday Darkside activities as brawling, stealing and murder, even Elias Carnegie had to watch his step. At a stroke, Scabble had dodged a beating from the wereman, and bought himself enough time to get rid of those cursed silks. Even with the Runners about, he could probably still sell them piecemeal on the street. Perhaps this affair could have a happy and profitable ending after all.

Buoyed by his narrow escape, Scabble set off for his dock-front office with a spring in his step. He strode through the darkness along the wooden decking, whistling a jaunty tune to himself. A dilapidated sign advertising the office of Scabble Trading, Inc, creaked in the salty breeze as Scabble fumbled with the key to the front door. He was just about to enter the building when the hairs on the back of his neck stood to attention for the second time that night.

Scabble peered out towards the end of the pier, where the shadows congregated beyond the reach of a fog lamp. A tall figure was silently watching him, his cloak billowing out over the water's edge.

"Who's there?" Scabble called out.

"Do I really need to introduce myself?" the man said, stepping into the light.

Scabble gasped. He was confronted by a pale, handsome man who leaned on an expensive ivory cane, a blood-red velvet waistcoat visible through the opening in his cloak. Although the man was smiling, his expression held all the warmth of an arctic wind. His heart sinking, Scabble wondered what higher power he had offended to deserve this run of luck.

"Mr Vendetta, sir!" he cried out. "It seems to be my day for meeting dignitaries. First Carnegie, and now you!"

"I would hardly classify that mongrel as a dignitary," Vendetta said sharply.

What on earth was Vendetta doing here? The richest man in Darkside moved in privileged circles of which Scabble could only dream. But Vendetta was more than just a businessman; he had long maintained a reputation as one of the most feared men in the borough. Rumours abounded that he possessed dark powers – there were whispers of bodies found face down in the grounds of Vendetta Heights, puncture marks in their necks. Vampire or not, Scabble knew one thing: if Vendetta was here, he was in serious trouble.

"Quite a surprise seeing you in these humble surroundings, sir."

Vendetta inclined his head, an amused expression on his face.

"Did you hear the bells, sir?" Scabble tried again, a little desperately. "Thomas Ripper's died. I'll wager the Bow Street Runners are already on the streets."

Vendetta chuckled mirthlessly. "Come, come, Scabble, there's no need to be afraid. You won't be needing their protection. If I wanted you dead, you'd already be so. As it happens, I want you to help me."

"Help you, sir? Me?"

"Desperate times call for desperate measures. And they don't get more desperate than you, Scabble. As it happens,

Thomas's death has greater implications than you could possibly imagine. It means time is running out on a long-term plan of mine, and I find myself in need of a man with your particular . . . *talents*."

"Of course, sir," Scabble said, trembling as Vendetta drew near, "if there's anything I can do to help you, I'd be honoured."

"I rather thought you might be. Now, listen closely. . ."

With that, Vendetta whipped his cloak around Scabble's shoulders, and enveloped him in darkness.

1

No matter how long she thought about it afterwards, Kate Riley could never quite explain why, on a chilly November morning, she decided to follow Jonathan Starling. At the time, it seemed such an insignificant act; Kate could never have imagined how it would turn her world upside down.

The very fact that she had noticed him in the first place was unusual – after all, Jonathan excelled at being forgettable. Kate had first caught sight of him on the games field three years earlier. He was standing apart from the others near the touchline, shivering in the cold, hands bunched up in the long sleeves of his shirt. His hair made frantic distress signals in the breeze. Though the game was in full progress, no one seemed aware that Jonathan was there – the PE teacher nearly trod on his foot as he ran past to blow up for a foul. Half a field away, waiting for her hockey game to start, Kate felt as though she was the only person who was aware of the boy's existence. On the way back to the changing rooms, she pointed Jonathan out to her friends and asked if any of them knew him. They shrugged and shook their heads, then changed the subject.

From that moment on, however, Kate maintained a secret surveillance on Jonathan. Why she was so interested, she couldn't say: it wasn't as though he was good-looking. He drifted around the school grounds like a ghost, rarely talking to anyone. Sometimes he was in lessons, sometimes he wasn't. Sometimes Kate would see him walk out through the school gates in the middle of the day, right under the noses of teachers. Sometimes a tiny woman would pull up in a car by the front entrance and drive him away. It seemed that no matter what he did, no one took any notice.

And then, one day, he vanished completely.

Normally, the school would have been in uproar over such an occurrence, but the reaction to Jonathan's disappearance was muted. The police came to school to interview the pupils, only to learn that most of them had never even heard of the missing boy. Kate kept her mouth shut, and pretended she didn't know him either. Before long Jonathan's name had been removed from the registers, and he had become little more than a quiz question: "Remember that weird lad who went missing? Did they ever find him? What was his name again . . . something Johnson, wasn't it?"

It would be nearly a year until she saw him again, twelve months of Kate's life which had gone by depressingly slowly. Her mum and dad seemed to be fighting all the time. Kate wasn't sure what they were even arguing about – something to do with her dad going out late at night. At first she thought he was having an affair, until one night he returned home bleeding and covered in bruises. Kate's mum angrily accused him of breaking old promises; he snapped back that it was something in his nature, and that she could never understand. As the shouting got louder, Kate closed her bedroom door and turned up her stereo.

One morning she woke up to discover that her parents had been too busy arguing to do the ironing, and by the time Kate had sorted out her uniform she was late. She reached school to find the hallways and corridors already deserted, her footsteps echoing loudly in the hush. Nearing her form room, Kate raced through a set of double doors and rounded the corner only to crash headlong into another person. The impact sent her sprawling to the floor. Before she could react, a hand pulled her up firmly, and she found herself face to face with Jonathan Starling.

Kate stared at him, open-mouthed. To her mounting amazement, his face broke into a grin. She had never seen him smile before.

"Sorry about that," he said, a trace of amusement in his voice. "I tried to get out of the way, but you were a bit too quick for me. You OK?"

"Fine," Kate managed, her cheeks flushed. "My fault. It's just, I'm really late. . ."

"Yeah. Me too," Jonathan replied, looking unconcerned.

"It's my first day back, and I've kind of forgotten where everything is."

"You were away for a while." She phrased it as a statement, not a question.

"Yeah."

"Good to be back?"

Jonathan shrugged. "I guess." He looked around, sizing up his surroundings. "We should go. After all, you're only getting later."

He turned to leave.

"It's nice to see you again, Jonathan," Kate blurted out.

At the mention of his name, he stopped and looked back at her, the smile replaced by a look of curiosity.

"Thanks," he said finally, and continued off down the corridor.

One thing was abundantly clear: wherever Jonathan had been, it had changed him. Whereas in the past he had seemed somehow lost and overlooked, there was a new confidence and self-belief about him that Kate noticed, even if no one else did. He still kept his distance from the other pupils, but now she sensed that this was by choice. Even so, every time their paths crossed he smiled and gave her a quiet hello.

One morning Kate was staring out of the window, lost in a daydream, when she saw Jonathan walking purposefully across the playground towards the far end of the school grounds. Wherever he was going, it had nothing to do with lessons. What was he doing? Kate couldn't resist it – excusing herself to go to the toilet, she left the classroom and hurried after him.

It was cold outside, and a biting wind gnawed at Kate's bare legs. She walked as quickly as possible across the playground in pursuit of Jonathan. If he'd turned round at any time, it would have been obvious she was following him, but he didn't seem to care. He headed down the side of the sports hall and behind the back of the building – a favourite hideout for smokers and amorous couples. Hugging the side of the wall, Kate came to the corner and peeped around it.

Behind the sports hall, a girl was waiting for Jonathan. She was short, with flaming red hair. Pretty, Kate conceded, in a striking sort of way. Even though she was their age, the girl wasn't wearing a school uniform – instead she was muffled up in a thick black overcoat, with matching hat and gloves. There was a grave expression on her face.

Jonathan called out and greeted the girl. They hugged one another, but not comfortably. Whoever this girl was, Kate thought, she wasn't his girlfriend.

"I got your note," he said. "I'm still surprised, though. What are you doing here, Raquella?"

"I could ask you the same question," the girl replied.

"Thought that would be pretty obvious," Jonathan said wryly. "I'm back at school."

The girl looked enquiringly at the building behind her.

"Never had the chance to go to school myself. What's it like?"

"Tedious," replied Jonathan. "Especially the double French lesson waiting for me this afternoon. On the plus side, no one's tried to kill me for three months, which is a record. But then, you didn't come all this way to talk to me about school."

Around the corner, Kate was perplexed. The quip about people trying to kill him should have been ridiculous – so why did she have the strange feeling Jonathan wasn't entirely joking?

The redhead took a deep breath. "I came here to warn you. You're in grave danger."

"Danger?" Jonathan laughed. "Here? The worst thing that can happen to me here is detention, Raquella."

"You don't understand," the girl said. "Two nights ago Thomas Ripper died. Darkside's ruler is no more."

"What's that got to do with me?"

At the word "Darkside", something had stirred within Kate, the faintest glimmer of recognition somewhere in the back of her mind. She shook her head and tried to focus on the girl's story.

"I was working late at Vendetta Heights when the Blackchapel Bell begin ringing. At once I heard the front door slam, and saw my master's carriage driving off into the night. He didn't return until the early morning, and spent all of the next day locked in his study. I tried to see him, but he refused to talk to me. The only servant he spoke to was

Mr Pelham, the butler. Last night he went out again, and I haven't seen either him or Mr Pelham since."

"Maybe Vendetta got peckish and went looking for some necks to chew on," Jonathan said. "He is a vampire, after all, Raquella. Did you expect him to leave you a note?"

Vampire? Kate blinked with surprise. It was surreal to hear the word in the everyday surroundings of her school. Was it another joke? One thing was for sure: the girl wasn't laughing.

"Yes, thank you for reminding me of that fact," Raquella retorted icily. "Actually, Vendetta always tells me when he's going somewhere. He doesn't just disappear. I checked his wardrobe – some clothes were missing. The clothes he wears in Lightside. And when I cleaned the study this morning, I found this in the grate."

She handed Jonathan a scrap of charred paper. He looked at it, frowning.

"This is the address for this school!"

Raquella nodded. "I don't know what my master is planning, Jonathan, but he's coming for you. That's why he refused to speak to me – he knew that I would try to warn you."

To her horror, Kate felt a sudden tickling sensation in her nostrils. Ducking back round the corner of the sports hall, she clamped a hand over her mouth and stifled a sneeze. The conversation halted abruptly – Kate stood stock-still, barely daring to breathe. There was a long, wary pause.

"So what am I supposed to do?" Jonathan said eventually. "Go to the police and tell them a vampire's after me?"

"Come back to Darkside with me," urged Raquella. "We'll go and see Carnegie. You'll be safer there, and it will give us enough time to find out what Vendetta wants with you."

"I can't just run off to Darkside!" Jonathan protested. "Dad'll kill me! He made me promise to give school a real go this time."

"Stay here, and there's a good chance that Vendetta will kill you. I know my master's ways all too well, Jonathan. I wouldn't have come all this way if I wasn't certain your life depended upon it."

The maid's solemn words hung in the crisp winter air. Her pulse racing, Kate felt everything hanging in the balance as Jonathan struggled to come to a decision. Then he sighed.

"I never did like French, anyway. Let's get out of here."

2

Jonathan quickly led Raquella out of the school grounds, and they began the short journey back to his house. The maidservant walked in silence, wrapped up in her own thoughts. Though he was pleased to see Raquella again, Jonathan never felt entirely at ease around her. She was so sensitive that he constantly found himself saying the wrong thing. At times Jonathan found it easier dealing with Carnegie's violent mood swings than the defensive little maid. Even as she walked by his side, her cheeks reddening slightly in the wind, he got the sense that Raquella was somehow disappointed that he had needed persuading to go back to Darkside.

However, for all her prickliness, once again she was risking Vendetta's wrath to help Jonathan. Given the number of times Raquella had defied the vampire, it was a minor miracle that he hadn't drained her as he had the rest of his servants. On the other hand, given the cold brutality with which Vendetta treated Raquella, it was equally amazing that she chose to stay in his service. Some relationships, Jonathan decided, were just a mystery.

They were passing by a row of shops on the main road, where boxes of fruit and vegetables were marinating in exhaust fumes on the pavement outside. There was the wail of a siren, and a police car hurtled past them – Jonathan had to force himself not to duck behind something. Although he had been back on Lightside for three months, he still couldn't believe the police weren't after him. The last time he had seen Raquella, they had broken into a mansion in Kensington, in search of a precious Darkside artefact known as the Crimson Stone. In the end, they had narrowly escaped the mansion with their lives, only for the stone to disappear back in Darkside.

Jonathan had wanted to continue the search for the stone, but there wasn't a single clue to go on. Instead, he had reluctantly decided to stay in Lightside to face the music. After all, having made a dramatic escape from a London police station, Jonathan was now both a missing person and a suspect in an unsolved robbery. If it hadn't been for the fact that his dad was waiting for him at home, he probably wouldn't have gone back at all. But he had taken a deep breath, crossed back, and waited for the police to arrest him.

Nothing happened. No one asked him any questions. No one said anything. No one even knocked on the door. Jonathan settled back into his bedroom, re-enrolled at his old school, and began trying to lead a normal life. Weeks after his return, he found an article mentioning the robbery buried deep within a London newspaper. It said simply:

> *ROBBERY BREAKTHROUGH: Police investigating a break-in at an exclusive address in Kensington arrested several unnamed suspects at an address in south-east London yesterday. Detective Horace Carmichael, who was leading the investigation, said that he was satisfied with the outcome of the operation, and that the police were not looking for any further suspects.*

There were no more details. Jonathan didn't know what to make of it – he knew for a fact that his accomplices, the burglarious Troupe, were safely back in Darkside. He remembered Detective Carmichael, and his assistant Sergeant Charlie Wilson, from his interview at the police station. While the young sergeant was just like all the other policemen Jonathan had encountered, Carmichael was different – an enigmatic hunchback who gave the impression that he knew more than he was letting on. And yet here he was saying the case had been solved.

Maybe Carmichael had believed his story. Maybe he was embarrassed that a boy Jonathan's age could escape from his grasp. Maybe, like so many other Lightsiders, he had simply forgotten about him. Whatever the reason, Jonathan was relieved that the police wanted nothing more with him.

As they turned off the main road and towards the leafy

avenue where he lived, Jonathan had to admit that the last few weeks hadn't actually been that bad. After a year of almost constant danger, it had been nice to relax and spend time doing things he hadn't done for a while: lounging around watching rubbish television; downloading songs from the internet; chatting to his dad and the family's closest friend, Mrs Elwood. They tried to avoid talk of Darkside, mostly because it proved a painful reminder of the absence of Jonathan's mum. Though Theresa Starling had vanished in the rotten borough over ten years ago, both Jonathan and his dad still nurtured the hope that she was alive, and that they would see her again.

The Starlings' house boasted the signs of a recent makeover – the windows had been cleaned, and the peeling paintwork redone. Jonathan walked up the driveway and into the house. Inside the front room, his dad was sitting in an armchair, leafing through a large leather-bound book. On the table next to him, a skin was developing on top of an untouched cup of coffee. Mrs Elwood was reading a magazine on the sofa, her tiny legs folded up beneath her.

Alain looked up with surprise as Jonathan entered the room.

"What are you doing back here?"

"Someone wanted to see me," Jonathan replied, and stepped to one side, revealing Raquella.

Alain took off his spectacles. "I suppose we'd better have a chat, then."

*

They gathered around the kitchen table and ate an awkward lunch. Raquella's appearance was the first time Darkside had touched the Starlings' lives for several months, and Jonathan could feel the tension in the air. Raquella was cold and withdrawn, Mrs Elwood openly hostile. The tiny woman rolled her eyes and tutted as Jonathan outlined the situation. Only Alain seemed unaffected by the atmosphere, chewing thoughtfully as he finished his lunch. Then he swallowed.

"No," he said.

Jonathan blinked. "Sorry, Dad?"

"I said no. You're not going to Darkside. You're going to stay here like we agreed."

"Didn't you hear what Raquella said? Vendetta's coming after me!"

"So she thinks. A scrap of paper, some missing clothes – it could mean anything, son."

"My master has never forgiven Jonathan for crossing him," Raquella said quietly. "Believe me when I say he means to do him harm."

"And if that turns out to be the case, we'll deal with it here," Alain replied.

"How?" Jonathan said, his voice rising. "This is a *vampire* we're talking about, Dad! I know that we've managed to beat him before, but at some stage our luck's going to run out."

"And if he stays, he'll be placing you *all* in danger," Raquella added. "The best thing for everyone would be for Jonathan to return to Darkside with me."

"You'll forgive me if I'll be the judge of what's best for my family," Alain snapped, the sharpness of his tone startling Jonathan. "I am his father, after all."

"Alain's right, Jonathan," Mrs Elwood interjected. "Do you really think you're going to be safer in Darkside? Listen to yourself, for heaven's sake!"

"I don't get it," Jonathan said. "You never had a problem with me going back before!"

Alain leaned forward. "I've let you go to Darkside in the past either because you were in danger and I couldn't look after you, or I thought it might help us find your mother. But now I *can* look after you, and this has nothing to do with Theresa. I refuse to turn our lives upside down again on the basis of what that wretched vampire may or may not do."

As the maid sighed and pushed away her plate, Alain turned to her.

"Raquella, I am grateful that you've come all this way to warn Jonathan, and I know that by doing so you've put yourself in danger. But you have to understand – I care about Jonathan's safety too, and right now I think the best thing he can do is stay here in Lightside with his father."

Raquella rose stiffly from her chair. "I understand completely, Mr Starling. We have different concerns. I'm a Darksider, Jonathan's part-Darksider, and—"

"And I'm not?" Alain finished, his gaze hardening.

There was a pause.

"No," the maid replied eventually. "You're not. As I said, we have different concerns. Good day to you all."

With that, she walked out of the kitchen.

"Wait, Raquella!" Jonathan called out, but the only reply was the sound of the front door closing. He turned and glared at Alain.

"Good one, Dad," he said sarcastically.

As Mrs Elwood coughed uncomfortably, Alain collected up the lunch things and carried them over to the sink.

"There are limits, Jonathan," he said quietly, and left the room.

Later that night, the Starling house remained sullenly, stubbornly silent. Mrs Elwood had long since made her excuses and left, leaving the main combatants to their cold war. After the fight in the kitchen, Alain had retreated into his study, and hadn't reappeared. Jonathan had spent the rest of the day moping round the house, feeling equally restless and angry. Though deep down he could understand why his dad had forbidden him from going to Darkside, it didn't mean that Jonathan agreed with him.

Now he was lying on his bed, flicking through an old comic book. He knew that he should probably go to bed, but there was no way he was going to sleep yet. It wasn't just that he was annoyed with Alain – he also had a horrible nagging suspicion that, somewhere in Lightside, Vendetta was closing in on him.

A rattling sound at the window made him jump. As Jonathan put down his comic book, another rattle followed hot on the heels of the first. He stole cautiously over to the window and pulled it open, shivering as a draught of November air blew into the room. He looked down to see Raquella standing in the shadows of his back garden, a handful of stones in her palm.

"What are you still doing here?" Jonathan hissed.

"I told you," she called up. "You have to come with me!"

"You heard what my dad said! He'll go mad if I go behind his back!"

Raquella rolled her eyes. "We've coped with worse than that, haven't we? You know I'm right. Why else are you awake?"

Jonathan bit his lip. The last thing he wanted to do was defy his dad. But if Raquella was right, then by staying here he was placing both Alain and Mrs Elwood in danger. More than that, the pull of Darkside was making his heart pound and the blood swell in his veins. He could almost hear the raucous streets bursting into life with the onset of night-time. In one way, Raquella was right: Alain could never understand that feeling.

"Hurry up! It's freezing down here!"

Jonathan took a final look back at the bright, inviting warmth of his bedroom, and then slipped out of the window, down the drainpipe and into the night.

3

Jackdaw Square was carefully stashed away in the south-west corner of Darkside like stolen booty. Four rows of plush terraced housing surrounded a small garden, which was guarded from the public by spiked iron fences. The affluent residents were taken from the higher echelons of Darkside society – elevated above the hovel-dwellers of the Lower Fleet by several lifetimes of robbery and plunder, they were only one forged will away from being able to afford a mansion on Savage Row.

At three o'clock in the morning, the respectable silence was disturbed by the sound of horses' hooves. A carriage rattled into the square, pulling up by a house on the north side. The carriage door opened, and two teenagers climbed down on to the pavement. One – a girl – spoke briefly to the driver, and then walked up the steps towards the house. As the carriage sped away, the other – a boy – examined his surroundings in the glow of the street lamps.

"Very nice," Jonathan said. "Don't know why you had to send the carriage away, though."

Raquella looked back from the door. "Not everyone wishes to advertise their connections with my master, especially at this time of night. And there is someone here we should speak with."

Who, exactly, she didn't seem inclined to tell him. From the moment they had reached the end of Jonathan's road to find a carriage waiting for them, the maid had been tight-lipped, refusing to answer his questions. Judging by the crest on the side of the carriage, Jonathan gathered they were travelling in one of Vendetta's private vehicles, but the route they had taken to Darkside remained a mystery. When he tried to look out of the window to see where they were headed, the maid reached over and firmly pulled down the blinds.

"Hey! Why did you do that?"

"This is a route my master often uses when he has business on Lightside. By rights I shouldn't be aware of it – were it not for the special circumstances, I would have travelled another way. There is certainly no need for you to know about it."

As the carriage rolled on through the night, Jonathan felt inclined to disagree. Ensconced in the warm interior of the carriage, he experienced a more comfortable journey into Darkside than he had imagined was possible. Even with the blinds drawn, Jonathan knew the exact moment they crossed into the rotten borough – he could feel it in the very marrow of his bones. His head went dizzy, as though he had stood up too quickly, but it was an exhilarating rather than unpleasant sensation. He slumped back in his seat and closed his eyes, smiling. In the past, crossing from modern London to Darkside had caused him pain and sickness, but his body had adapted to the extent that it now welcomed the change. As they continued through Darkside, Jonathan could feel the borough reaching out to reclaim the senses it part-owned: the thick, rancid odour that drifted up from the sewers in search of tender nostrils and soft stomachs; the distant screams and shouts of alarm; the acrid taste of smoke in the air.

However, even from the confines of the carriage, Jonathan was increasingly aware of something new, a nervous edge to the atmosphere that he hadn't experienced before. If he hadn't known better, he would have called it fear.

Still feeling energized by the crossing, he now ran up the steps to join Raquella, and peered at the bronze plaque by the side of the front door.

"Dr Hugo La Mort," he read aloud. "Who's that, then?"

"A friend of my master's. Vendetta visits him before every trip to Lightside. He may know something that could help us."

Jonathan gave Raquella a sideways glance. "'Friend'?"

"Of sorts," she replied defensively.

The maid pulled the bell rope, and a series of chimes sounded within the house. They stood in silence, expecting to hear footsteps, but the front door opened without warning.

"*Oui?*" said a quiet voice, through a crack in the door.

"Dr La Mort?" Raquella asked. "It is Raquella – Vendetta's maidservant. Please forgive the intrusion at such a late hour, sir, but I was wondering whether you could help me with an urgent matter."

"The hour is of no consequence, child," came the soft reply, in a voice tinged with a European accent. "I am still working. Death and disease do not sleep; therefore, neither do I. Come in."

The door opened, revealing a peculiar-looking man. He was small, with an outsized, egg-shaped head sparsely covered with strands of slicked-over hair. Two tiny legs struggled to support the weight of his portly belly, giving him the appearance of a Russian doll. The doctor's shirtsleeves were rolled up, and he was wiping his hands on a towel. Ushering Jonathan and Raquella inside the house, he locked the door behind them, and drew heavy bolts across the top and bottom of it.

"You must forgive my precautions, but in this borough one can never be too careful, *non*? Keeping a nice house requires not only pounds and shillings, but constant vigilance."

With this declaration, Dr La Mort led them up a flight of steps to the second floor. The upstairs study they entered was a shrine to biology: bookshelves sagged under the weight of old medical textbooks; black-and-white anatomical diagrams covered the walls; by the window, a display cabinet was crammed with glass jars filled with murky liquid. At the far end of the room, a floor-length curtain had been drawn from one wall to the other.

After the cold air outside, it was unnaturally hot inside the room. As Jonathan unbuttoned his coat, Dr La Mort settled himself neatly into an armchair and made a grand gesture, like a showman about to introduce his next trick.

"So, child," he addressed Raquella, "what ails you? What need have you of Dr La Mort's assistance?"

"My health is fine, sir. It is my master I have come to see you about. You are close to him, are you not?"

The doctor raised a wry eyebrow. "I would not say your master has many *amis*. There was James Ripper, of course, but we all know what happened to him. Such a tragic affair. But it is true that I am Vendetta's doctor, and from time to time we have discussed matters over a glass of brandy. In many ways, he is a great man. With his knowledge of the body, he could have added much to the field of medicine."

Struggling with the notion of a vampire doctor, Jonathan tried to stifle an incredulous laugh.

Dr La Mort fixed him with a sharp look from across the room. "That amuses you? Child, there is nothing funny about medicine."

"Please forgive my friend," Raquella cut in. "He does not know Vendetta well enough to appreciate his gifts. I came here tonight because my master has unexpectedly disappeared. Naturally, I am concerned about his whereabouts, and hoped you might be able to shed some light on the matter."

The oddly shaped little man sat back in his chair, thoughtfully pressing the tips of his fingers together. Jonathan's attention drifted over to the glass jars in the display cabinet next to him. Idly he tapped one of the jars, and was startled when there was a movement within the liquid. Jonathan took an instinctive step back. Whatever was inside, it was alive.

"*Mais oui*," Dr La Mort said finally. "Vendetta came to see me two nights ago. He desired certain special infusions that only I make."

"Infusions?" queried Raquella.

"From time to time, there are some Darksiders who wish to travel beyond the borough's edge. For a small price, I provide medicines that help counter the side effects of the journey."

"Did he say why he wanted to go to Lightside?" Raquella pressed.

Dr La Mort shook his head. "It did not seem right to ask, *non*? He was very impatient – demanded that I make the infusions right there in front of him. When he had what he needed, he swept out of the door with barely an *au revoir*. The only thing I can tell you, child, is that wherever your master has gone, it is on a matter of the utmost urgency." The doctor stood up. "Now, please forgive my rudeness, but I must return to my work."

Smiling, he reached behind the curtain and pulled out a

white porcelain bowl. Looking down into it, Jonathan saw a collection of sharp implements staining the porcelain with blood. His stomach turned. The doctor carefully rummaged through the bowl before selecting a large scalpel. The blood on the blade glistened in the soft light.

Dr La Mort slowly passed the scalpel beneath Jonathan's nose, whispering, "Tell me, child, how can a doctor – even one as skilled as I – hope to succeed without tools such as these? There was a time, years ago, when I possessed the finest medical instruments in Darkside. Then no operation was too complex. I was an artist, and now I am forced to hack and slice like a *butcher*!"

As Jonathan swallowed nervously, Raquella pulled at his sleeve.

"Thank you so much for your help, doctor," she said hastily. "We should be leaving now."

"You don't want to stay?" The doctor leaned towards them. "I could show you some of the marvels of the human body."

"Another time, maybe. . ."

"It is really getting late. . ."

"Of course, you are free to go whenever you please," Dr La Mort whispered. He gestured towards the window. "But the weather is closing in fast. You would be much more comfortable here, *non*?"

Following the doctor's gesture, Jonathan saw with a sinking heart that fog had descended upon Jackdaw Square, a grimy blindfold obliterating the other houses from view.

The only thing he could make out was the wispy glow of the street lamps.

"It's all right – we're not far from home," Jonathan lied, retreating towards the door.

"We'll let ourselves out," added Raquella.

The pair of them backed out of the study and hurried down the stairs, desperately fighting the urge to run. Following them to the landing, Dr La Mort watched every step, the scalpel still in his hand, menace in his eyes. Jonathan felt the doctor's gaze boring into the back of his neck like a drill. As he tried to draw open the bolts on the front door, he found that his hands were shaking.

"Quickly, Jonathan," Raquella murmured, out of the corner of her mouth.

The top bolt was sticking fast. He pulled on it again, harder, but it wouldn't budge.

"Having problems, child?" Dr La Mort called down. "Let me help you."

"No! We'll be fine, really. . ." Jonathan assured him.

"It is no trouble for me."

The strangely shaped man began stepping slowly down the stairs towards them, scalpel raised in his hand. Abandoning any pretence of calm, Jonathan slammed his shoulder against the door and threw all his weight into working the bolt free.

"Jonathan!" Raquella shouted, as Dr La Mort reached the bottom step.

With a final furious effort, the bolt slid free, and they

tumbled out on to the street, racing away from the house. The fog had fallen as swiftly as a portcullis, and Jonathan could barely see beyond the fingers on his outstretched arm. Realizing that he was running blind, he came to a halt by the side of a wall.

"Raquella?" he called out.

The sound of his voice echoed around Jackdaw Square, but the maid didn't answer. Jonathan was about to shout even louder when a scraping noise behind him made him turn. Peering through the fog, he saw to his horror that the bricks in the wall were rumbling and shifting into a shape. He took an instinctive step back, but it was too late. Suddenly, the bricks formed into a large hand, which thrust out towards Jonathan and grabbed him by the throat.

4

Maintaining a savagely tight grip around his neck, the hand raised Jonathan up into the air, forcing him to stand on tiptoes. With his throat held, he was unable to cry for help, and trying to struggle out of the vice-like grasp was futile. Jonathan watched helplessly as the wall continued to writhe, the patterns in the brickwork taking on increasingly defined, recognizable shapes – a burly arm, a heavy boot. Eventually, with a loud rumble, a creature pulled itself free from the wall and stared down at him.

It was at least eight feet tall, and composed entirely of blackened, sooty bricks – even down to its uniform of jacket, trousers and boots. Despite its ungainly frame, the creature's movements were smooth, bricks scraping into position with surprising fluidity. Now it craned its head towards Jonathan, subjecting him to a blank, stony gaze.

"You shouldn't be here," the creature said, soot spraying from its mouth like saliva. Its voice was deep and grating, as though someone was running a washing machine filled with pebbles and slate.

"Please. . ." Jonathan gasped, his feet scrabbling to touch the pavement. "I can't breathe. . ."

The creature ignored him. "Who are you?"

"Jonathan . . . please let go. . ."

The pressure on his neck was unwavering, inhuman. Jonathan could feel his limbs weakening as the oxygen drained from his body. Still the creature held him.

"What are you doing hiding in the fog? Looking for a purse to cut?"

"No! I was visiting someone. Please. . ."

Jonathan's head was swimming, black spots exploding in front of his eyes. From somewhere on the other side of the square, he dimly heard the sound of hurried footsteps.

"Wait, officer!" a female voice cried out.

The creature's hand snapped open, dropping Jonathan to the pavement with a crash. He clutched at his neck, fighting a rising tide of nausea. Suddenly Raquella was kneeling next to him.

"Jonathan! I lost you! Are you all right?"

Unable to speak, he nodded numbly. The maid rose and turned towards the creature, which was watching the two of them impassively. Through watering eyes, Jonathan saw her greet it with a respectful curtsy.

"Good evening, sir. What is the problem here?"

"It's late to be wandering the streets. Too late for respectable citizens."

"It's my fault, officer," Raquella replied. "I was conducting urgent business on behalf of my master – I had forgotten that the Bow Street Runners were abroad."

The creature gave her a hard stare. "The Runners are *always* abroad when Darkside's throne is empty."

"I know – I should have remembered. It will not happen again, I promise."

There was a rippling movement across the Runner's shoulders that Jonathan guessed was some sort of shrug.

"It'll be your funeral if it does."

With that, the creature stepped back into the wall, its limbs dissolving with a rumble into the brickwork, until it had been swallowed up entirely. Jonathan climbed gingerly to his feet and ran a hand incredulously over the now-smooth wall.

"What the hell was that?" he asked, looking back at Raquella.

"A Bow Street Runner," she replied thoughtfully. "Part of the Ripper's personal police force."

"It moved through the *wall*, Raquella."

The maid nodded. "They're brick golems. They can move faster through walls than you or I can run. With no Ripper on the throne, some Darksiders might see an opportunity to seize power for themselves. The Runners tend to make them think otherwise."

"No kidding," Jonathan replied ruefully. "I thought Darkside was feeling a bit jumpy – I can see why now. This has been quite a night. First that nutty doctor, and now this."

Raquella bit her lip. "I'm sorry, Jonathan. I should have warned you about the Runners – I truly forgot. Let's get out of here – the sooner we catch up with Carnegie, the better."

She walked swiftly away, the fog threatening to swallow her up.

"You sure you want to keep going on foot?" Jonathan called out dubiously. "Wouldn't it be safer getting a carriage?"

Raquella turned and said, with a hint of a smile, "Didn't you hear? The Runners are patrolling the streets. This is the safest Darkside gets."

"Tell that to my throat," Jonathan muttered, as he hurried to catch up with her.

As they exited the square and headed down a broad avenue towards the centre of Darkside, the dank curtain of fog began to lift, almost as suddenly as it had arrived. It revealed a warren of deathly quiet streets, as though the citizens of Darkside had been magicked away. From the arches beneath Eel Pie Viaduct, usually home to a bustling, argumentative community of beggars and cripples, to the distant, wild expanse of Bleakmoor to the north of the borough, there was no one to be seen. Even on the Grand – the epicentre of Darkside's nightly tremors – the pavements were empty. The unnatural stillness made Jonathan feel uneasy; he jumped when a carriage clattered hastily past him, the coachman whipping his horses into a frenzy.

Carnegie's lodgings were located above a funeral parlour on Fitzwilliam Street, a cankerous offshoot of the

Grand. Jonathan hauled himself up the familiar staircase, his feet automatically avoiding the loose step halfway up. At the top of the stairs, a landing led on to a thick red door marked with deep scratches. Jonathan marched up and banged on the door, but there was no reply. Beside him, Raquella shivered.

"What do we do now?" she said. "We can't go looking for him. There's no telling where he might be."

"Don't despair," Jonathan replied. He crouched down and ran a hand underneath the doormat, pulling out a dull metal key. "I spent enough time here to know where the spare key is."

Raquella frowned. "Could Elias not have found a slightly less obvious hiding place?"

"Do you really think he needs to?" Jonathan asked, turning the key in the lock. "You'd have to be nuts to break in here!"

A grey dawn was creeping in through the windows of the lodgings. Elias Carnegie was splayed out on the settee in his front room, fast asleep, one leg trailing out on to the floor. His waistcoat was unbuttoned, revealing a tired white shirt marked with stains. A battered stovepipe hat had slumped down over his face, muffling the wereman's loud snores. His left hand still clutched an empty brown bottle, and the floor around the settee was littered with a graveyard of gnawed animal bones. The entire room was steeped in a mood of sullen inertia as thick as the animal hairs on the furniture.

Surveying the scene, Raquella shuddered. "I think *you* should wake him up," she said.

Jonathan grinned. "No need. He smelled us coming up the stairs – didn't you, Carnegie?"

"You're a genius, boy," a voice rumbled from beneath the hat. "Now get out of here and let me sleep, before I decide I'm still hungry."

Jonathan winked at Raquella.

"He's missed me," he said.

Two hours later, and a weak winter sun was doing its best to illuminate the shabby surroundings of the lodgings. The wereman picked at his teeth with a claw while Jonathan and Raquella enthusiastically attacked breakfast.

"If you've come here because you're bored on Lightside and you fancy some more adventures, you've picked the wrong time, boy," he growled. "Damn, but Darkside is dreary right now."

"It's like a graveyard out there," agreed Jonathan, tearing the crust off a piece of bread and dipping it in his egg.

"Give me a graveyard any day," Carnegie muttered. "Always a chance of running into a wight or two for a bit of sport. Right now, everyone's so scared the Runners are going to nab them for something that they're taking a break from any criminal activities. Those walking hods are bad for business – I haven't had a new case in days."

"Yeah, I've already had the pleasure of meeting a Runner," said Jonathan. "We didn't exactly hit it off."

"They don't have the most developed people skills," conceded Carnegie. "But they are effective. So, if you haven't come for a day trip, why are you here?"

"I'm in trouble," said Jonathan. "I need your help."

The wereman sat back in his chair and eyed him suspiciously. "What have you done now?"

"Actually, Elias," Raquella cut in, "it's not Jonathan's fault. . ."

As the maid's story unfolded, Jonathan, well used to Carnegie's moody ways, expected the wereman to pace furiously up and down the room, peppering the air with oaths. He was surprised when Carnegie merely tilted back his head and listened quietly, nodding from time to time. When Raquella finished, the private detective smiled grimly.

"That master of yours has a thing about Jonathan, doesn't he?"

"Not many cross Vendetta and survive," Raquella agreed solemnly. "I don't think he will ever rest until he feels he has exacted his revenge."

"Well, it's not as though we haven't stopped him before. Boy, you look like you're sitting on a lit firework. What's the matter?"

"It's nothing really," Jonathan said cautiously. "Just that . . . this is usually where you shout at me for getting you into trouble."

Carnegie laughed gruffly, and playfully cuffed Jonathan around the back of the head. "Given how boring things are right now, I wouldn't have minded if you'd tweaked the nose of Jack the Ripper himself. Anything for something to do."

"So what now?"

The wereman stretched lazily. "Hmm . . . Raquella, you say that Vendetta refused to talk to you, but he did speak with the butler?"

"Mr Pelham? Yes, he was the only person allowed into the study, but I don't know what they talked about. As I said, I haven't seen either of them since."

"Well, let's go up to the Heights and find out if the butler saw anything."

"Go to the Heights?" Jonathan said dubiously. "I thought the idea was to keep away from Vendetta!"

"If Raquella's right, then Vendetta's on the other side of London – the Heights is the last place he'll look for you. Besides, it's a prime opportunity to nose around the place while the vampire's away, and I'm not about to miss out on that. Come on."

As the wereman punched his hat back into some sort of shape and rose to his feet, the sound of chattering voices drifted up from the street below. Carnegie looked out of the window and checked his pocket watch with a frown.

"What is it?" asked Jonathan.

"Forget my own head next," Carnegie muttered to himself. He looked up. "Change of plan. We'll go to the Heights after we go to the Tyburn Tree."

Jonathan was puzzled. "The Tyburn Tree? Why – what's there?"

The wereman flashed him a toothy smile. "In about half an hour, the new Ripper," he replied.

5

After the eerie quiet of the previous night, it was reassuring to see the streets now busy, the Grand reverberating to the familiar shouts of hawkers and the rattling procession of carriages. But there was a strained nature to the doorway deals and shady plots – heads turned to look over shoulders, while eyes glanced nervously at the nearest wall, as though the conspirators were fearful that at any moment a Bow Street Runner would explode forth.

Typically, Carnegie seemed immune to the atmosphere. Hands thrust deeply into his pockets, he barged his way into the stream of Darksiders flowing northwards along the Grand, carrying Raquella and Jonathan in his slipstream. Unusually for the borough, everyone appeared to be heading in the same direction.

By the side of the road, a newspaper boy had taken up a vantage point on top of an upturned crate, and was exchanging copies of his paper for coins.

"Get your *Informer* here!" he cried out. "Special early morning edition – Blood Succession begins today!"

Jonathan felt a tingle of excitement run along his spine. During his time in Darkside, he had heard tales of the Blood Succession, but it had never occurred to him that he would actually be there when one took place. Tradition dictated that the Ripper's successor was decided by a fight to the death between his children. The battle always took place in Lightside – apparently, as a reminder to Darksiders of the cowardly Londoners who had turned their backs on the blighted district during the time of Jack the Ripper.

A siege had erupted around the newspaper boy as – tired of paying for their newspapers – the denizens of the Grand had started simply snatching them from the bundle beneath his arms.

"'Ere! Gerroff!" the boy protested. "There's enough to go round! Hold yer horses!"

It was a futile protest: Jonathan heard the upturned crate crack under the pressure, and the newspaper boy toppled from view, his last copy of the *Informer* fluttering up into the air. Carnegie emitted a guttural chuckle.

"I'm surprised everyone's making such a fuss," he remarked cheerfully. "This Succession will be a doddle."

"You really think so, Elias?" asked Raquella.

"Simple arithmetic. Thomas Ripper had three children, didn't he? Lucien murdered his brother James years before the Succession, managing to break just about the only rule we've got in this blasted borough. If he shows his face in public now, he'll be lynched. Which only leaves Marianne as a rightful heir. Forget the Blood Succession – this is going to be little more than a coronation."

Although in one way Jonathan hoped the wereman was right, another part of him wasn't so sure. Even though he had nearly died at the hands of Lucien in the past, the fact remained that the Ripper's son was the only man in Darkside who knew what had happened to Jonathan's mum. The unpalatable truth was that, if Theresa Starling was still alive, Jonathan needed Lucien to be too – at least long enough to tell him where she was.

"Now Thomas's Succession," Carnegie continued, "that was a *real* event. He had three brothers, all as strong and as mean as he was. They fought in Lightside for two days without stopping, and by the time Thomas had polished them all off he was half-dead himself. Rumour has it he crawled back to Blackchapel on his hands and knees. No one thought he was going to pull through, and there was nearly a riot in the streets. Then the Runners stepped in and had a sharp word with some of the rabble-rousers. Funnily enough, everything went quiet after that."

Up ahead, the crowd was surging west at the crossroads on to Pell Mell, the broad thoroughfare that led towards the Rippers' ancestral home. As the turbulent flow of humanity threatened to sweep them away, Jonathan and Raquella kept close to Carnegie, sheltered from pushes and jostling elbows by the tall wereman's presence.

Pell Mell was an unerringly straight avenue lined by two rows of stunted trees with scorched, arthritic trunks. The horizon was dominated by Blackchapel's bleak outer walls, which had protected its nefarious inhabitants from the sullying stares of its subjects since the days of Jack the Ripper. Only the tip of an ornate spire gave any clue to the presence of a building beyond the wall. Each slab of stone was the colour of night, and must have weighed tons. To Jonathan, it seemed as though only time itself, the passing of century after century, could wear the barricade down.

With each approaching step, the walls loomed higher, and the mood among the Darksiders descended into one of subdued awe. Before the Blackchapel gates, Pell Mell broke out into a wide plaza, in the centre of which was a strange wooden structure on a raised platform. The crowd milled around it expectantly.

Jonathan nudged Carnegie. "What's that? Where's this Tyburn Tree?"

"You're looking at it."

Jonathan had been expecting some kind of an imposing oak or beech tree with branches large enough to interrupt the skyline. Instead he found himself looking at three upright timbers rising into the air, joined at the top by a flat wooden triangle made up of three beams. As he peered more closely, Jonathan could see lengths of rope hanging forlornly from the horizontal beams.

"Doesn't look much like a tree to me," he murmured.

Carnegie nodded. "It's only a nickname, boy. Don't you recognize a gallows when you see one?"

Suddenly the dangling ropes assumed a much darker significance. Jonathan shivered. "I didn't realize Darksiders could be executed."

"Only during the Succession," the wereman said nonchalantly. "Why do you think everyone's so jumpy? The Runners find that making public examples of a few citizens makes it easier to keep everyone else in line."

"You mean people come and *watch*?" Jonathan asked incredulously.

"Well, Darksiders generally prefer a bit more of a battle, but you can usually rely on getting a decent crowd for a hanging." Carnegie chuckled. "Nearly made it up there myself during Thomas's Succession, when I was a little 'un. One of the Runners caught me stealing apples, and was very close to stringing me up."

"For stealing apples?"

Carnegie grinned, baring his huge incisors. "Technically, the apple *tree* was in Blackchapel, and the Runners get a little testy if you start clambering around the walls there. . . Here we go. Looks like we're about to get under way."

As Jonathan watched, four Bow Street Runners clambered up on to the wooden platform, which trembled beneath the weight of their stone footfalls. When each guard had taken up a position on a corner of the platform, a man with long, groomed white hair took to the stage. His clothes bore the trappings of fanciful ceremony, and a golden chain of office glinted around his neck.

"Who's that guy?" Jonathan whispered.

"Aurelius Holborn," replied Raquella. "He's the Abettor – the Ripper's right-hand man. He runs Darkside during the Blood Succession."

"The way I hear it," Carnegie murmured out of the corner of his mouth, "Holborn's been running this place for a lot longer than that. While Thomas Ripper has been laid up in bed these last few years, apparently it was the Abettor making most of the decisions."

Watching Holborn stride regally across the platform, Jonathan could believe it. As the Abettor stood calmly gazing out over the masses, the hush deepened with expectation.

"Citizens of Darkside!" Holborn proclaimed, in a powerful voice that carried easily out over the throng. "Following the sad passing of our iron ruler, Thomas Ripper, we gather here today to signal the beginning of the Blood Succession. As tradition dictates, those children born of the departed Ripper may step forward and fight one another for the glorious honour of Darkside's throne. Can anyone present lay claim to such a birthright?"

For a few seconds nothing happened. Then an amused female voice broke the silence.

"I suppose that would be me."

A figure emerged from the front of the crowd and moved gracefully up the steps of the wooden platform – a slender woman with dyed purple hair and porcelain skin. Jonathan recognized her all too well – it was Marianne, bounty hunter, and the only daughter of the Ripper. Their paths had crossed many times before, almost always with ill consequences for Jonathan. Even so, he couldn't bring himself to hate her as perhaps he should.

As she took her place beside the Abettor, Holborn bowed smoothly and kissed her proffered hand before turning back to his audience.

"By the powers vested in me," he boomed, "I recognize Marianne's right to enter the Blood Succession. Does anyone else wish to press their claim?"

Heads turned in the crowd as Darksiders looked about for another challenge. Caught up in the tension, Jonathan felt his heart beat faster in his chest. Even Carnegie looked engrossed.

The seconds seemed to stretch on for hours, until Holborn finally looked up and announced, "With no other challengers, there can be no Blood Succession. It therefore falls to me to proclaim Marianne as the new. . ."

"HOLD!" a voice cried out.

The crowd gasped as one. There was a commotion at the side of the gallows, and then a hooded figure limped on to the stage. A Runner took a menacing step towards the stranger, only for Holborn to restrain him with a raised hand.

"Declare yourself, stranger. Who dares interrupt this coronation?"

"I would have thought that would be obvious," the man replied. He drew back his cowl, revealing a gaunt face with closely cropped black hair. "My name is Lucien Ripper, son of Thomas, and I stand before you as the rightful heir to my father's throne."

As uproar broke out around him, Lucien stood unbowed, his lip curling with disdain as he surveyed the crowd. Jonathan was suddenly reminded of the last time he had seen that face, when Lucien had taunted him about his mother. Hate surging through his veins, Jonathan made to push forward towards the stage, only for a strong hand to grab his arm.

"Hold fire there, boy," Carnegie murmured. "Not the right time."

"Brother-killer!" came a shout from the throng.

The jeers rose to a crescendo, and a bottle came flying from the crowd, missing Lucien's head by an inch. Immediately, the Runners rumbled forward to the front of the platform, forming a stone barrier between the crowd and the Rippers. Holborn held his hands up for quiet, and called out in a booming voice: "The next person to interrupt this ceremony will find himself hanging from the Tree."

Immediately the din abated. Having let his threat hang in the air, the Abettor continued in a softer voice.

"Every man and woman present knows of the shameful deed in Lucien's past, and that it is a stain on his claim that can never be removed. That being said, who here can deny that he is Thomas's son? Who here can refute his birthright to take his place in the Succession? I cannot, and I will not. If the Rippers look down upon Lucien and find him unworthy of the throne, then may Marianne's sword find the centre of his heart. The Succession will judge, not us."

There were mutters and grumbles amongst the crowd, but all took care to keep them out of the Runners' earshot.

"And so," Holborn declaimed, "Lucien and Marianne will fight one another to the death to determine who shall become the next Ripper – as their father did before them, and his father before that. As the neutral judge of this combat, I will decide the location in Lightside and inform both parties. Until that combat, the Runners' word is law."

At an abrupt signal from the Abettor, the stone golems stepped down into the audience and began herding people away from the platform. As the crowd began to drift reluctantly back towards the centre of the borough, Jonathan saw that only Marianne and Lucien had remained on the stage, brother and sister staring coldly at one another, death on their minds.

6

"I don't believe it!" Raquella said indignantly, as they retreated back along Pell Mell. "How can Holborn allow Lucien to take part in the Succession after what he did?"

"I guess the Abettor wants people to know that he's not taking sides," Carnegie replied. "I can't imagine Lucien would have stayed in hiding for ever. Marianne might as well put an end to him once and for all." He glanced at Jonathan. "You all right, boy? Thought you were going to climb the Tree at one point."

"Yeah, I lost control for a minute. I'd forgotten how much I hate Lucien."

"No shame in that," the wereman said staunchly. "I don't care how many rogues and scoundrels there are around here – if Lucien takes the throne, Darkside will descend into hell. Mark my words."

With that sombre thought ringing in their heads, they turned off Pell Mell and quickly left the milling crowds behind them, making for Savage Row, the exclusive street on which Vendetta Heights proudly stood. As they crested the low hills to the north of the borough, the air became crisper and cleaner, and they found themselves navigating a narrow, winding road that skirted round a succession of large mansions. As ever, Jonathan struggled to believe that Savage Row could exist in such a place as Darkside, when the vast majority of its inhabitants lived in such squalor. The street was one long, extravagant boast. Despite the lateness of the year, the trees lining the Row maintained their leafy canopy, as though the usual rules of nature didn't apply to them.

The adrenaline that had coursed through Jonathan's system at Lucien's reappearance had slackened, replaced by a creeping sense of apprehension. For all Carnegie's reassurances, Jonathan still couldn't believe that turning up at the Heights was a wise idea. The events at the Tyburn Tree had only underlined the strangeness of the vampire's disappearance. If Vendetta had chosen to go to Lightside in the middle of a Blood Succession, when the next Ripper was about to be decided, then it had to be for a reason of utmost importance. But how on Darkside could that involve Jonathan?

The road suddenly levelled out, leading on to a straight, broad avenue. The trees were so thick that, despite the early hour, the way ahead was gloomy. The chatter that had sustained them this far abruptly stopped, and they continued in silence. The avenue ended at a high, moss-covered wall and a forbidding set of iron gates. Looking beyond that, Jonathan could see a sprawling Gothic building with scarred brickwork: Vendetta Heights.

Raquella pushed open the ivy-clad gates and began briskly crunching up the long gravel driveway. Jonathan followed slowly behind, nervously taking in his surroundings. Although this was the fourth time he had visited the Heights, he still felt the same apprehension he had felt on his first visit. More than anything else, it was the stillness of the place, the absence of sound and life. In front of the house, even the fountain of the small crying child had been turned off, leaving the statue rubbing its eyes for no reason.

"This place gives me the creeps," Jonathan muttered to Carnegie. "What if it's a trap or something?"

The wereman stopped in his tracks and stared pointedly at Jonathan. "What are saying, boy? You think Raquella's sold you up the river? That lass may be a handful, but I've lost count of the times she's put her neck on the line for you. You couldn't dream of a better friend."

"I was only saying—" Jonathan began, his face reddening.

Carnegie shook his head sadly. "Lightsiders. No sense of loyalty."

The maid was ringing the front doorbell, examining the windows for any sign of movement within the mansion. She turned back to her companions, frowning.

"Mr Pelham should definitely be here by now," she said.

With nothing stirring inside the building, Raquella

brought out a heavy iron key from the folds of her uniform and unlocked the door. The hall beyond was dingy, with the cold, stillborn air of a crypt. As Carnegie strode eagerly after Raquella, casting an appraising eye over the grotesque wooden friezes on the walls, Jonathan lingered in the doorway, unwilling to enter the building.

"Mr Pelham?" Raquella called out. "Are you there?"

The Heights remained silent.

"Doesn't appear to be anyone at home," mused Carnegie. "Why don't we split up and have a look around while we're here?"

"Split up?" Jonathan asked apprehensively.

"Boy, even you can't get into trouble in an empty house. It's not like there's going to be booby traps or anything. . ." Struck by a sudden thought, the wereman shot a questioning glance at Raquella, who shook her head. "OK – I'll take the upper floors; Raquella, you check out the servants' quarters. Perhaps our Mr Pelham is a heavy sleeper. Boy, the cellar is all yours. Shout if you find anything."

With that, Carnegie loped up the central staircase and disappeared down the first-floor landing. Raquella gave Jonathan a slight shrug, and bustled off into the adjoining room.

Though Vendetta was nowhere to be seen, there were reminders of his presence everywhere: in the lavish dining room, a single place had been laid at the end of a long table; in the cavernous library, a book lay open on the reading desk; in the study, a letter lay half-written, the pen still resting in the inkpot. At any moment, it seemed like the vampire might appear out of the gloom and resume his work.

Jonathan headed reluctantly to the back staircase, muttering to himself. The last thing he wanted to do was descend to the cellar, but he couldn't face admitting to Raquella that he was scared. Only pride kept him moving down to the lowest floor of the mansion. He pushed open the creaking cellar door.

The first thing he noticed was the cold – the atmosphere in the room was arctic. Only the faintest shards of light dared creep this far down, meekly illuminating a rickety table and a wine rack running along the far wall. Jonathan inched across the flagstones, his breath forming frosty clouds in the air. Like all the other rooms in the Heights, there was no sign of life, no spiders' webs or scuttling rodents. As he passed by the table, something brushed against Jonathan's foot. His heart pounding, he looked down.

It was a corpse's hand.

Jonathan yelled out with fright, stumbling backwards. At first he thought he had discovered Vendetta, but then he realized that the man was wearing the formal suit and buttoned collar of a servant. The body was stretched out on the floor underneath the table, a single telltale slice carved into the neck.

There was a commontion on the stairs, and Carnegie clattered into the cellar, brandishing a candelabra. The wereman skidded to a halt when he saw the corpse, and, observing no imminent threat, eyed Jonathan with bleak amusement.

"Ah. Well, I suppose I did tell you to shout if you found anything."

"It's not funny, Carnegie!"

"I know, boy." The wereman placed the candelabra down on the table and looked over the body. "I'm presuming that we've found Mr Pelham?"

"That's him," a female voice replied. Jonathan spun round to see Raquella standing in the doorway, sadly taking in the scene. The maid crossed the cellar and knelt down by the body, closing the butler's eyes. There was a calm acceptance about her behaviour, a reminder that this was not the first such dreadful sight she had witnessed in this house.

"Death seems to be an occupational hazard in this place," Carnegie said. "Your master is a real piece of work, Raquella."

"It is his nature," she replied quietly. "Vendetta has little choice in the matter."

"Really? How have you stayed alive all these years, then?"

The maidservant began to reply, and then stopped.

"Hang on a minute." Jonathan bit his lip, thinking. "What was he doing in the cellar? There's nothing here."

Carnegie nodded at the bottles of wine. "Maybe he was getting Vendetta a drink."

"I doubt it," said Raquella. "Since his illness I've barely

seen him touch a drop. I haven't had reason to come down here for months."

Jonathan knelt down and began inspecting the bottles near the butler's outstretched hand. The maid looked on nervously.

"Please be careful – those are the most expensive bottles in the mansion. If anything happened to them, my master would be furious. *Especially* that one – it's priceless."

"This one?" Jonathan's hand stopped by a dusty bottle on the bottom row of the rack. "Really? Oh well, Vendetta's never really liked me anyway."

He pulled the bottle out from the rack. As he slid it free, he saw a cord had been tied to the bottle's base. There was a loud click, and a part of the cellar wall beyond the rack slid to one side, revealing a pitch-black opening.

Jonathan stood up, brushing his hands clean. "Looks like Mr Pelham found more than he bargained for. Fancy a look inside?"

Carnegie passed him the candelabra. "Your discovery, boy. After you."

With a deep breath, Jonathan stepped into the darkness.

7

Jonathan moved slowly down a narrow corridor, holding the candelabra out in front of him like a shield. The candles flickered and shied in the draught, as though fearful of going any further.

"Everything all right in there, boy?" a gruff voice called out behind him.

"Yeah," Jonathan replied edgily. "There's a room up ahead."

He stepped cautiously through a doorway, and into the cramped confines of the chamber beyond. Measuring barely four paces by four paces, the secret room was little more than a cubbyhole. There were no windows set into the walls, and only two items of furniture: a clerk's bureau, and an accompanying high stool. On the surface of the bureau, a large black book was resting next to a small silver key.

Behind him, Jonathan heard the rustling of a skirt. Raquella took in her new surroundings with undisguised amazement.

"You really didn't know this was here?" asked Jonathan.

She shook her head, bewildered. "The Heights are riddled with secret passageways and rooms. I've seen only a handful, and even those I discovered by accident. I thought Vendetta went down to the cellar less than I did."

"One of the advantages of being a creature of the night," Carnegie remarked wryly from the doorway. "More time for skulking around."

The low ceiling had forced the wereman to remove his stovepipe hat, and he stooped slightly as he entered the room. Wiping his nose on his sleeve, Carnegie appraised his surroundings.

"For some reason, I was expecting something a little more grand," he concluded. "Flocks of bats. Walls drenched with blood. A coffin, at the very least."

Jonathan went over to the bureau and picked up the silver key, inspecting it in the candlelight.

"Any idea where this might go?" he asked.

Carnegie shrugged. "There's a lot of locks in Darkside, boy. Fancy trying every one?"

"Guess not."

As he tossed the key back on to the bureau, Jonathan felt a tug on his sleeve. He turned to see Raquella tracing her fingers over the cover of the black book.

"It's not the key that's important here," she breathed. "It's this!"

The maid hurriedly settled down upon the stool and

opened the book. As she reverently turned the crisp parchment, Jonathan saw that the pages were filled with rows of names and numbers written in dried brown ink in small, copperplate handwriting.

He frowned. "What is it?"

Absorbed in the pages, Raquella barely seemed to register his question. "This is Vendetta's ledger for his private bank. It contains the account details of his most wealthy and important clients: every bribe they received, every stolen item they've bought. Occasionally I've seen him carrying it, but I've never had the chance to look inside it. I thought he left it at the bank."

Carnegie raised a hairy eyebrow. "Very interesting. I'd imagine there's a few dirty secrets in here," he said. "Quite a lot of people would like to get their hands on this, I'll bet."

"Quite a few have tried," Raquella replied quietly. "Where do you think he got the ink from? Blood dries brown, you know."

Jonathan shuddered. Knowing Vendetta, he could have guessed that the ink had a gruesome origin. Even so, the thought of the vampire spending his nights alone in this room, scratching out his accounts in his rivals' blood, sent a tremor down his spine.

By contrast, Carnegie seemed intrigued by this revelation. Taking the ledger from Raquella, the wereman turned to the last page, running a craggy finger down to the most recent payments.

DATE:	FROM:		TO:
2/11/DY119	Baron von Hesse	£60	Lorcan Bracket
3/11/DY119	Thomas Horne	£5	Josiah Bartlemas
5/11/DY119	Yann Belmont	£25	Una Hawkins
6/11/DY119	G. Vendetta	£100	Dexter Scabble

The wereman banged his fist down upon the table, making both Jonathan and Raquella jump.

"Scabble!" he barked angrily. "I should have throttled that louse when I had the chance!"

"You know him?" asked Raquella.

"Can't be a private detective in Darkside without knowing Dexter Scabble. He's a low-rent thief who operates out of Devil's Wharf. I was questioning him on another matter when the Blackchapel Bell started ringing. Had to let him go – much to my regret."

"That night was the fourth of November," Raquella said thoughtfully. "Judging by the dates in the ledger, two days later Vendetta was paying him £100. Which is hardly loose change."

"It's not *that* much," said Jonathan.

"Our currency is a bit different to yours, boy," Carnegie growled. "Round here, a hundred pounds would buy you a small chunk of the Grand." The wereman glanced at Raquella. "What is your master doing paying all this money to a bilge rat like Scabble?"

"I wish I knew, Elias," the girl replied. "Vendetta's never even mentioned his name to me."

"One thing's for sure," Carnegie remarked. "This wasn't a charitable donation. There's something fishy going on here, and I've got a nasty feeling it involves the boy. Let's go and see if Mr Scabble can shed any light on the subject." The wereman grinned. "I'm sure he's been missing me."

They left the still confines of Vendetta Heights at once – pausing only for Raquella to find a canvas bag, into which Jonathan slipped the ledger. As they passed through the gates of the mansion and back on to Savage Row, Jonathan exhaled deeply, relieved to have left the Gothic estate. Carnegie flagged down a passing hansom cab and ordered the driver to head south. The cab trundled through the dingy afternoon to the sound of the driver muttering dark, unintelligible threats to himself.

As they travelled south, the air developed a salty tang, and seagulls cried as they banked and wheeled through the sky. In the distance, Jonathan could make out the river lapping wearily against a series of wooden jetties, and the outline of a steamer ship heading out into open water to deliver its illicit cargo. They had arrived at their destination: Devil's Wharf.

Scabble Trading, Inc, was situated at the lowest, dirtiest end of the wharf. Despite the proud sign above the door, the office was little more than a wooden shack teetering on the edge of the waterfront. Even the breeze gusting in off the river couldn't shift the smell of rotten fish guts, and the general atmosphere of seediness that hung over the area.

Without bothering to knock, Carnegie barged through the shack's front door and into a threadbare office. A small, wiry man sprang out of his chair.

"What the blazes?" he cried.

Carnegie gave him a toothy grin. "Hello, Dexter. Told you I'd be seeing you again."

Jonathan blinked. Though Dexter Scabble had tried to present himself as a well-to-do businessman, it wasn't a very convincing façade: his shoes didn't match, his tatty waistcoat was missing buttons, and there was a large white stain on his bowler hat that Jonathan guessed was a seagull's dropping.

"Carnegie!" exclaimed Scabble. "I told you, those missing silks were nothing to do with me!"

Even as he spoke, Jonathan noticed the thief's eyes flick guiltily over to the three large crates piled up in the corner of the office.

"Calm down," the wereman replied mildly. "As it happens, that's not why I'm here. The boy wanted to have a chat with you. I'm just keeping him company."

Scabble glanced over to the window, as though weighing up whether to make a break for it, before suspiciously resuming his seat.

"I wanted to ask you about Vendetta—" Jonathan began.

"Never heard of him," Scabble replied automatically.

"Then how come he's just paid you a hundred pounds?"

Scabble's eyes narrowed. "What's that got to do with you?"

"It's your choice, Dexter," Carnegie growled, cracking

his knuckles ominously. “Either you can talk to the boy, or you can talk to me. I warn you, though – his manners are a damned sight better than mine.”

“You can’t threaten me!” protested Scabble. “The Succession is on – the Runners will be here faster than you can say ‘Tyburn Tree’.”

“Maybe,” mused the wereman. “But we’re an awfully long way from the Grand. How many teeth do you think you’ll have lost by the time they get here?”

Scabble leaned back in his chair. “A persuasive argument, Carnegie. You’re quite the negotiator.”

“And you’re quite the hustler. Why is Vendetta paying you all that money? What’s the scam?”

Scabble affected an injured expression. “A hustler? I’m hurt! I’m just a humble businessman trying to make ends meet. The transaction between Mr Vendetta and myself was an entirely legitimate one. And, might I add, a private one. I don’t see why I need to tell you anything more.”

Carnegie leaned in closer over the desk, digging his claws into the woodwork. “Let me explain things for you. Vendetta’s disappeared, and he’s after Jonathan here. As much as the boy can be a pest, I’ve grown accustomed to having him around – and I’m not going to be very happy if he turns up in a gutter without any blood in his veins. Given that you’re now such good pals with the vampire, I thought you might be able to shed some light on what ‘Mr Vendetta’ is up to.”

Scabble pushed his bowler hat up and scratched his forehead.

"All right," he sighed. "Listen, Vendetta did come and see me the night Thomas Ripper died. He wanted to procure a couple of items in a hurry, and thought I might be able to help him. It just so happened that they were in stock in one of warehouses along the docks, so two days later I went to the Heights to deliver them. It was all very amicable, I swear to you! Well, as amicable as things get with Vendetta, if you get my meaning. . . I was barely in his study for five minutes – to be honest, I'm not even sure he was listening to me. He kept looking at his watch, all impatient. When he got what he wanted he cut me off mid-sentence and got old Archie to chuck me out."

"Who, Mr Pelham?" asked Raquella.

Scabble snorted with laughter. "When we were growing up in the No'penny Poorhouse I knew him as plain old Archie. Last time I heard, he was still at the poorhouse, him and his niece Clara. P'rhaps that's why 'Mr Pelham' wouldn't let on he knew me – maybe he thought Vendetta might not like his butler having such humble origins. Archie was certainly worried about something. He was all sweaty and nervous, like a fellow who's about to pull a caper only to realize he hasn't got the bottle. In fact, maybe you should go and ask Archie Pelham some questions, instead of barging in here and bothering an innocent man like me."

Carnegie looked uncomfortable. "I don't think anyone's

going to be bothering Mr Pelham now. One final question: what was Vendetta buying from you?"

Jonathan was surprised when Scabble burst into high-pitched laughter.

"Do you take me for a fool, Carnegie?" he said. "You can beat me black and blue if you want, but the worst punishment you can deal out would be a picnic compared to what would happen if Vendetta found out I'd betrayed him. I've told you all I can. Gentlemen, I bid you good day. Feel free to take up any further matters with my associates."

Dexter Scabble dipped into his pocket and brought out a small whistle. On a shrill blast, three burly men dressed in striped blue and white sailors' shirts crashed into the office, bulging forearms crossed.

"Show them the door, boys," said Scabble.

8

Given the strange exchange she had witnessed between Jonathan and the redheaded girl, Kate wasn't entirely surprised by the empty chair in her classroom the next day, or the silence that greeted Jonathan's name on the register. But she was disappointed. After much thought, Kate had decided to confront Jonathan with what she had seen and heard behind the sports hall. She was curious how he'd react: perhaps he would be angry; maybe he'd think she was crazy. Maybe she *was* crazy – but Kate couldn't deny the connection she felt with him, a connection that demanded she find out what was going on.

Only now there was no one to ask. Jonathan had vanished again. As before, there was no outcry. The teachers didn't respond to his absence with the usual inquisitions, while Kate's classmates were too preoccupied with their own dramas to notice: worrying about exams, falling out and making up with their friends, trying to get over their hopeless crushes. If Jonathan's parents were worried, there wasn't any sign of them around school. It was as though he had been a figment of Kate's imagination.

At the same time, things weren't getting any easier at home. Her parents were fighting over smaller and smaller things, the arguments and recriminations becoming ever more bitter. Her dad was going out alone every night now, returning home only to shower and sleep. With his torn clothing and bruised face, he looked leaner and tougher than Kate had seen him before, and at the same time somehow more at ease with himself. As the fighting worsened, Kate retreated into herself, protected by the thickness of a bedroom door. The mystery of Jonathan Starling was a welcome distraction.

She was about to decide her next move when events at school overtook her. Kate was chewing on the end of her biro, trying to untangle her thoughts for an English essay, when the teacher stood up and cleared his throat, heralding an announcement.

"OK – listen up, everyone. I've had a call from Justin Starling's dad. Apparently he's not well at the moment, and the doctor's not sure how long he's going to be off school. Obviously we're in the middle of some extremely important coursework right now, and it's vital that he has the necessary notes. It would be great if one of his friends could take the notes round to his house – I'm sure he'd be delighted to see people. Who here's friends with Justin?"

There was a deafening silence. Slowly Kate raised her arm. "It's Jonathan," she said. "I'll take it."

She noticed one of her friends casting a quizzical look in her direction, which she ignored. The teacher gratefully laid a sheaf of papers down on her desk. "Yes, of course. Jonathan. How silly of me. The address is on top of the sheet."

After school, Kate avoided her friends and hurried through the drizzle towards Jonathan's house – which, as luck would have it, was quite close to hers. Given that the houses on his street were all large, detached buildings that must have cost a small fortune, Jonathan's home didn't quite fit in: it was a little more careworn, a little more vulnerable than its neighbours. To Kate, that seemed somehow fitting. The lights were on in the front room, but the rest of the house was dark.

Sheltering from the rain beneath the cover of a large tree on the other side of the road, Kate was suddenly struck by indecision. Although she had promised to deliver the notes, she was now reluctant to walk up the driveway and knock on the door. What if Jonathan was actually ill – what would he think about a stranger turning up on his doorstep? What if all of this was just her imagination running riot? What if there was no mystery?

As she watched the house, two figures appeared in the front room. One was the tiny woman Kate had occasionally seen picking Jonathan up from school, and a man she guessed had to be his dad. Though she couldn't hear what they were saying, Kate recognized two people arguing when she saw it. The woman seemed distressed, laying a hand on the man's arm as though she was trying to persuade him to stay, but he shook his head firmly. The man disappeared from the room, appearing outside the house some five minutes later, swathed in a long black coat. Bowing his head under the onslaught of the wind and the rain, he strode off into the evening. Kate was about to follow him when she saw the tiny woman standing in the doorway, staring straight at her. Startled, Kate turned and raced down the street in the other direction, the coursework notes forgotten.

Back in the safety of her bedroom, as she changed out of her sodden clothes and wrapped a towel around her hair, Kate felt a little foolish for having run away, but there was something about the woman's stare that had unsettled her. She didn't bother returning to the house to deliver the notes. Jonathan wasn't ill – she was sure of it now.

Two days later, and Kate was beginning to despair of finding Jonathan. The problem was, she didn't know anything about him: where he hung out, what he did, and with whom. Short of breaking into his house, there didn't seem anything more she could do. Kate was frustrated – she had snapped at her friends for no reason on the way to school that morning. If they thought she was acting oddly, they didn't mention it. They knew about the problems at home and silently drew their own conclusions.

The late November nights were rapidly drawing in, and during French, Kate's last lesson of the day, darkness folded itself around the second-floor classroom. Above her head, a strip light buzzed like a bee as it battled to illuminate the room. Sitting next to the window, Kate caught a glimpse of a movement down by the school gates. She looked down to see a silver car drive up through the gloom to the front entrance. A man got out of the car and walked briskly into the building.

Kate tried to focus on irregular verbs. A few minutes later a boy came into the classroom to deliver the teacher a note. She read it, raising an eyebrow.

"Kate? The headmaster wants to see you after school."

Thirty pairs of eyes turned towards Kate, thirty minds speculating on what terrible crime she had committed. There were a couple of low, mocking whistles. Her cheeks burned with the attention, and she was relieved when the final bell rang.

She walked slowly through the turmoil of the home-time rush to the headmaster's office, and settled in a chair in the reception room outside. As she waited, the shouts and footsteps gradually died away, until the last straggler had packed up his PE kit and wandered out of the school. The only sound was the faint oompah of the orchestra practising in the theatre on the other side of the school grounds.

Eventually the door to the office opened, and the headmaster appeared. Mr Holmes had never spoken to Kate before; for five years he had been little more than a distant figure on the stage during assembly, his booming voice echoing around the hall. As he ushered her inside the office, Kate noticed that for once he seemed unsure of himself, nervous almost. A blond-haired man turned in his seat, subjecting Kate to a piercing gaze. He was handsome, in a cold way, and he knew it.

"Kate," the headmaster said, "this is Richard Starling, Jonathan's uncle. He's here on behalf of his brother Alain, who's suffering from some health problems. Mr Starling has some questions he wants to ask you."

"What sort of questions?"

"Well, to begin with," the blond man said sharply, "where is he?"

"At home, isn't he?" Kate stalled, thinking quickly. "He's ill."

"No, he isn't," the man said. "Jonathan's gone missing – again. My brother's health isn't strong enough for him to come down to the school, so he asked me to try and find out what's going on. It's a good job I did. It doesn't appear that your headmaster was even aware that my nephew had vanished, let alone where."

"We know that you're a friend of Jonathan's," Mr Holmes cut in, tugging at his collar, "and that you volunteered to take him some coursework notes. Did you see him at all, or anything unusual? It could be important."

Kate bit her lip, facing a real dilemma. If Jonathan was in danger, she didn't want to lie about what she had overheard. On the other hand, there was something profoundly wrong about this situation. The atmosphere in the room was too tense, the blond man too impatient for a concerned relative.

Also, he looked nothing like the man Kate had seen in Jonathan's house – there was no way they could be related, let alone be brothers.

"I forgot to deliver the notes," Kate said finally. "I didn't tell anyone because I didn't want to get into trouble. I haven't seen Jonathan for days. If he has disappeared, I don't know where."

The last of which was true, at least. Kate stared straight ahead at Mr Holmes, aware of the other man's icy stare boring into her skin. The headmaster nodded, seemingly relieved by her answer.

"And if he contacts you – or you hear anything at all, you'll tell me?"

She nodded.

"Thank you, Kate. That will be all. As I told you, Mr Starling, Jonathan is a most irregular pupil. The school can't be held responsible for. . ."

Kate quickly shut the office door behind her, glad to escape the room. She walked out into the corridor, her heart pounding, and leaned against the wall. Without the chatter and laughter that echoed throughout the day, the building felt horribly empty. Notices pinned to the board flapped forlornly in draughts which seemed to come from nowhere. Kate shivered.

She was about to pull on her coat when there came a thud from the headmaster's office. Kate stepped hesitantly over to the door and listened, but all she could hear were low murmuring sounds. She shook her head. What did she think might be happening? All this stuff with Jonathan was making her go crazy. Kate was about to walk away when the door handle turned and the blond man strode out of the office. Behind him, Kate caught a glimpse of Mr Holmes slumped in his seat.

"Hey!" she shouted. "What's going on? What have you done to him?"

"Nothing that need concern you," the man snapped, advancing upon her and grabbing her arm tightly. Even through the sleeve of her school blouse, Kate could feel the chill of his hand.

"You're hurting me!" She squirmed. "Let go!"

"All in good time," the man murmured quietly. "Tell me where Starling is."

"I already told you: I don't know."

"You're lying," he said flatly.

"So are you," Kate shot back fiercely. "You're not his uncle. I don't know what you said to Mr Holmes, but I don't believe you. What did you do to him?"

It was at that moment she caught sight of the reddish smear of blood on the man's lip, and suddenly he didn't need to answer. With a sickening lurch in her stomach, Kate was reminded of something Jonathan had said behind the sports hall. At the time it had seemed like a bad joke, but now. . .

"I know who you are!" She gasped. "You're Vendetta. But Jonathan said you were a . . . you can't be!"

"A vampire?" The man grinned, revealing two elongated

incisors at the front of his mouth. "Whatever gave you that idea?"

It was too much to take in. Kate felt dizzy.

"But that's impossible," she murmured. "There's no such thing!"

"Really? I have to say, I expected you to have a slightly more open mind. After all, Kate. . ." She flinched as Vendetta leaned in closer to her, continuing in a whisper: "There's Darkside blood in you too. Diluted, weak, but there. I can almost *taste* it."

"I don't know what you're talking about," Kate replied. Her pulse was racing even as she spoke, as though the vampire's words had stirred something deep within her.

"Perhaps not," breathed Vendetta. "Not all Darksiders are proud of their heritage. Which parent has been keeping secrets from you, I wonder?"

Kate felt an explosion of rage within her chest. With a piercing scream, she wrenched her arm free with a strength she'd never thought she possessed. Vendetta tried to grab her, but Kate was already sprinting down the corridor.

She ran blindly, not conscious of the direction, spurred on by the urge to put distance between herself and Vendetta, up flights of stairs and through gloomy hallways. Kate dared not glance behind her, for fear of seeing the vampire on her heels. Though she couldn't hear him, she could feel his presence, was horribly aware of his silent pursuit.

After clattering through a set of fire doors on the first

floor, Kate skidded to a stop, a burning pain in her side. She'd never run so fast and so far before. As she caught her breath, she became aware of the discordant sound of the orchestra floating up from the hall below her. They had to be the only people left in the school. If Kate could reach them, she'd be safe! Bracing herself for one final effort, she hurried down the nearest flight of steps back towards the hall.

The brash chorus of trumpets and trombones were getting louder now. The sound had never been more welcoming. Avoiding the dangerously open spaces of the main corridor that led down to the hall, Kate ducked into a side room, a technology workshop instantly recognizable by its ever-present perfume of glue and sawdust. The room was pitch-black, wheels and lathes lying dormant in the darkness. On the other side of the room was a door leading to the main hall.

Sighing with relief, Kate walked up and tried the handle.

"It's locked, I'm afraid."

She whirled round, heart in her mouth. Vendetta stood in the shadows by the window. The vampire didn't seem out of breath – in fact, Kate wasn't sure if he was breathing at all.

"HELP!" Kate shouted, but at that moment the orchestra roused itself into a cacophonous finale of crashing cymbals that drowned out her cry. As Vendetta advanced, she backed across the workshop, until she bumped up against a workbench. As she scrabbled around for a weapon, her

9

Carnegie didn't hesitate. With a snarl he grabbed hold of Scabble and hurled the little man in the direction of the sailors. They had just enough time to bundle him out of the way before the wereman's charge – an onslaught of teeth and claws that managed to engage all three of them.

The tiny office struggled to contain the combatants: the windows rattled with every punch and the wooden walls creaked with every curse. As he scanned around for a weapon with which to help Carnegie, Jonathan spotted Scabble crawling out through the door on his hands and knees. He raced across the room and grabbed hold of one of the little man's legs, dragging him back inside the cabin.

"No!" Scabble cried, kicking out wildly.

Jonathan had pulled Vendetta's ledger from his bag, and was about to bring the book down on the thief's head when a large weight crashed into the side of him. Jonathan hit the floor hard, his landing only partially softened by Scabble himself. Dazed, still clutching hold of the ledger, Jonathan caught sight of an earring flashing in the light, and a tattoo of a mermaid etched on weather-beaten skin. An arm was pressing down across his chest, pinning him.

As Jonathan's head began to clear, a leering, scarred face filled his vision. Over his assailant's shoulder, Carnegie was occupied by the other two sailors, trading vicious slashes for their barrelling forearm blows. Jonathan was on his own.

With his free arm, the sailor pulled out a belaying pin from his belt – a long wooden club with a handle. He raised it above his head, his earring gleaming.

"Sweet dreams, laddio," he said.

Suddenly Jonathan knew what to do. With a giant effort he forced his left arm free, reached up and yanked the earring from the sailor's ear. The sailor screamed, clutching his bloodied lobe. With the grip loosened, Jonathan twisted his body and followed up with a swift knee to the groin. His assailant crumpled like an accordian, allowing Jonathan to roll free.

The pandemonium showed no sign of relenting. Carnegie had disposed of one of the sailors, and was now attacking the other. Scabble was lying winded on the ground, immobile.

"Get the girl!" he called out weakly to his henchmen.

In response, the sailor with the bleeding ear got to his feet and went after Raquella, who had taken up a position behind Scabble's desk. Jonathan raced after the man and tried to rugby tackle him, only for the sailor to brush him off with a trailing arm. Jonathan's nose exploded with pain – then, through his tears, he saw Carnegie step between Raquella and the sailor.

For a couple of seconds neither the wereman nor the final sailor moved. Then, without warning, Carnegie stepped up and unleashed an earth-shattering roar inches from the sailor's face. As the man blanched with horror, Carnegie picked him up and hurled him through the window overlooking the river. There was a scream, and then a splash as the sailor hit the water.

Suddenly it was very quiet, and very still. Carnegie glanced across at Jonathan, his eyes narrowed. "You all right, boy?"

Jonathan nodded, holding his nose, which was bleeding profusely. The wereman strode over to Scabble and lifted him up off the floor. He bunched a hairy fist.

"OK, OK!" Scabble cried out, shielding his face with his hands. "I'll tell you everything! It was a moonstone!"

Carnegie's brow furrowed. "What was a moonstone?"

"Vendetta's order. It's a kind of quartz . . . rare. . . I stole it direct from a steamer that had just come in from the east."

"What did Vendetta want with it?"

"He didn't tell me," the thief sobbed. "That's all I know, I swear!"

Carnegie relented, dropping Scabble into a forlorn heap on the floor. "For once, I'm going to take you on your word. For your sake, I hope I don't regret it. We'll see ourselves out. Oh, and Dexter?"

The thief looked up groggily, to see Carnegie nod at the stolen crates in the corner of the room.

"I'll be back to collect those silks when the Succession's over. Keep an eye on them for me, will you?"

Outside, the shadows were starting to lengthen along the waterfront. Carnegie buttoned up his overcoat and inhaled a deep breath of the salty air, apparently invigorated.

"That was fun," he said brightly.

Jonathan eyed the wereman grumpily, dabbing at his nose with a bloody handkerchief. "For you, maybe. You weren't the one having your nose broken."

"What are you complaining about, boy? A broken nose gives a man character. Darkside women don't trust a man with an unmarked face."

"I'll take your word for it."

Raquella was staring out over the murky waters, lost in thought. She turned back to look at them. "I've never heard Vendetta talk about moonstones before. I can't imagine what he'd want with one."

"Me neither," Carnegie agreed. "Let's go see what some old friends can make of it."

The offices of the *Darkside Informer* were located in the tanning district on the east side of the borough. Pedestrians hastened through the shadows of giant factories. Industrial chimneys weaved a blanket of poisonous smoke over the rooftops, the smell of leather so thick it left an aftertaste in the mouth. Even by the low standards of Darkside, this was a grimy, insalubrious area.

Which made it the perfect hideout for the journalists of the *Informer*. They were marked men in the borough: Darksiders liked their secrets to stay secret. On his previous visits to the newspaper, Jonathan had found the office to be a gloomy, furtive place, where every stranger was greeted with suspicious glances and watchful eyes. This time, however, as the three of them entered the building, he heard an unfamiliar sound above the rumbling of the printing presses: laughter.

Jonathan came into the main office, and blinked with surprise. The dismal atmosphere had vanished. The boarded windows had been freed up, allowing the room's occupants to see the Darkside skyline as it retreated into early-evening darkness. The coal stoves had been lit, and were pumping waves of warmth out into the office. Gas lamps burned fiercely on every desk, chasing away the shadows and casting a rosy glow on to the faces of a group of journalists as they sat around swapping stories. Engrossed in a particularly long tale, not one of them acknowledged the new visitors.

The storyteller was a man Jonathan knew well: Arthur Blake, editor of the *Informer*. Always comfortable recounting his great deductions and daring deeds, the rotund man had his audience in the palm of his hand. Despite the fact that

Jonathan was never entirely sure that Blake's stories were true, he couldn't help himself: he laid the bag containing the ledger down on the nearest desk and crept closer to listen in.

". . . So no one knew what had gone on, but when I looked over the photographs of the wedding I noticed that one of the footmen in the background had a rather familiar mole on his left cheek. It was none other than Owen Galbraith, the celebrated thief!" Arthur paused, allowing his audience to digest this fact. Then he sighed, and continued hurriedly: "Sadly, by that time Galbraith was long gone, and so was the bride's necklace, but it made for a first-rate exclusive. . ."

At the back of the room, Carnegie snorted loudly with amusement. "You're quite the detective, Blake. Ever thought of taking it up full-time?"

Arthur looked up, his chubby face breaking into a smile. "Carnegie!" He hopped out of his chair and waddled over to shake hands.

"Everyone seems remarkably cheery in here," the wereman muttered, as Arthur enthusiastically pumped Jonathan and Raquella's hands. "Is it payday?"

"Better than that," Arthur laughed. "It's the Succession. With the Bow Street Runners out, a journalist's life becomes altogether easier. We can even walk the streets unharmed. Though we still have to get the edition out tonight." He turned and clapped his hands. "Back to work, everybody!"

The reporters drifted slowly back to their desks. When

Arthur spoke again, it was in a conspiratorial whisper. "Now, what can I do for you?"

"What do you know about moonstones?"

The portly editor raised an eyebrow. "As much as any man on my salary can be expected to. They're expensive minerals that have to be specially imported – they don't tend to turn up in the Lower Fleet, if you catch my meaning."

"What are they used for?" asked Jonathan.

"Mainly ornamental purposes: decorating mirrors, lamps, watches. . ."

"Doesn't sound like a typical Vendetta purchase," Carnegie rumbled.

"The vampire's involved?" asked Arthur.

"According to Dexter Scabble, and there's a payment in Vendetta's ledger to prove it," Carnegie replied. He turned to Jonathan. "Where is it, boy?"

"I left it over – hey!"

From nowhere, a boy had soundlessly crept up to the desk behind Jonathan and now sat idly flicking through the ledger, his feet propped up on another chair. The boy looked up and winked at Jonathan, who grinned with recognition. Harry Pierce was the son of James Ripper, who had died at his brother Lucien's hands. With James dead, Harry no longer had any claim to the Ripper's throne, and had instead settled down as a journalist at the *Informer*. Although at first Jonathan had despised Harry's airy, arrogant demeanour, he had come to respect the boy's bravery, and knew better than most that beneath his frivolity lay a serious soul who had never really recovered from the death of his father.

Not that this was easy to tell right now. Harry was beaming from ear to ear, completely unaffected by Carnegie looming over him.

"That's not yours to read, Pierce. I don't recall giving you permission."

"It's not yours to read, either," Harry retorted. "Did Vendetta give *you* permission?"

"We didn't have the opportunity to ask him," Raquella answered sharply. "My master is hunting Jonathan, and we have to find out why. All we know is that it is tied in with Thomas Ripper's death, and the moonstone Vendetta bought from Scabble."

"Hmm. . ." Harry mused as he pored over the ledger. "Interesting. You said something about moonstones being used in watches, right? Well, you might want to investigate this payment here."

Jonathan followed Harry's finger along the final page of the ledger to a small, innocuous payment above the Scabble entry:

DATE:	FROM:		TO:
3/11/DY119	Thomas Horne	£5	Josiah Bartlemas

"Bartlemas is a watchmaker on the other side of town," Harry explained. "And Thomas Horne, well, I hardly need to tell you who he is."

At the mention of the second name, Arthur Blake looked up sharply, brow creased in thought. "Incredible. I wonder that this means?"

"I thought it was interesting too," Harry said happily, blowing the fringe out of his eyes. Looking up at Jonathan and Carnegie's blank faces, he chuckled. "You don't know who he is, do you?"

"Not yet," Carnegie growled, "but if you don't tell us sharpish, there's going to be some unpleasantness."

"Really, Elias," Arthur tutted reproachfully, "I'd have thought that you would have recognized the name. Especially given the current circumstances. . ."

Carnegie groaned loudly and put his head in his hands.

"Who is it?" asked Jonathan. "What's going on?"

"Whatever it is," the wereman replied grimly, "it's bigger than I could have imagined."

"Oh," Raquella said suddenly. "I see."

"I don't!" Jonathan cried out. "Who's Thomas Horne?"

"Most Darksiders knew by him by his real surname," Harry added. "The one he took up after the Blood Succession. I called him Grandfather."

Jonathan started. Harry's grandfather was Thomas Ripper. Then it came to him – all the Rippers lived under assumed surnames until the Succession. Thomas Ripper must have grown up as Thomas Horne. And was still using that name to pay Bartlemas thirty years later. Carnegie was right – something very big was taking place in Darkside, and Jonathan was being inexorably dragged into it.

Harry closed the ledger with a merry thump. “Aren’t you glad you stopped by?”

10

The carriage clattered through the streets, its frantic progress a legacy of the mishaps and miseries that had befallen countless previous journeys through the Darkside night. On the Grand, it had swerved violently to avoid the urchins scrabbling in the gutters for dropped pennies, and in the twisted arteries of the Lower Fleet, the coachman had to keep his nerve to speed past a gang of desperate robbers lying in ambush. The horses whinnied and bucked their heads in protest, the lash of the whip on their flanks driving them onward.

Sandwiched between Carnegie and Raquella in the back seat of the carriage, Jonathan felt every bump and jolt.

"Are we nearly there yet?"

"Not far now," Harry answered, hidden from view by Carnegie's sizeable frame. "Bartlemas's shop is just a couple of streets away."

Harry had insisted on coming with them, mischievously mentioning something about an exclusive. Now he was squashed up by the window, trying to read through the ledger, waving the corner of the book dangerously close to the scowling wereman.

"You might want to put that away, Pierce," warned Carnegie. "If I lose an eye, you can bet that you will too."

"It'd almost be worth it," Harry replied excitedly. "This ledger is *incredible*. Anybody who's anybody is in here. For example, did you know that Eli Kinski was paying the actress Gracie Harcourt ten pounds a week? No wonder she can afford to live on Savage Row!"

"I'm sure Kinski's wife would be delighted to hear that," Raquella replied darkly.

"There's a shady deal on every single page," Harry said, shaking his head in wonder. "Vendetta could have blackmailed half the borough if he wanted to. But that's not all – look at this."

He awkwardly passed the ledger around Carnegie to Jonathan. "The name Josiah Bartlemas turns up on the third of every month. Same amount, always from Grandfather. Like clockwork."

"But what was he paying him for?"

"That's what we're going to find out, boy," Carnegie rumbled.

As the carriage sharply turned a corner, Jonathan's brow creased with consternation. There was something about the name Bartlemas that was bothering him – for some reason, he couldn't shake the feeling that he had heard it before.

"We're here," said Carnegie, and banged on the roof of

the carriage. The coachman hauled on the reins, bringing the vehicle to a halt at the crossroads of two deserted streets of terraced housing. Bartlemas Timepieces had set up an unassuming residence on the corner, its run-down wooden façade and dusty latticed windowpanes shying away from the street lamps. The shop floor was dark, a "Closed" sign hanging in the front door. On the first floor, a large clock face had been set into the wall, the second hand conducting a silent circuit around the dial. It was approaching half past eleven at night.

Carnegie approached the building and peered in through one of the windowpanes.

"It's shut," he said.

"You noticed?" Jonathan shot back.

The wereman pulled away from the window and glared at him. "Bartlemas's shop is always open. The clock never stops, the door never closes. He's famous for it. No – this isn't right. Maybe Vendetta isn't the only Darksider who's left town." Carnegie stopped, noticing Jonathan's frown. "What is it, boy?"

"I dunno . . . it's weird. . . I've just got this feeling that I've seen this place before."

"Unlikely. We've never been to this part of town. You must be confusing it with somewhere else."

"Yeah . . . perhaps," Jonathan said slowly, though he knew that wasn't it. He glanced up and down the street. "Shall we have a look inside, then?"

Carnegie swung a boot back to kick down the front

door, but Harry stopped him. Pulling out a set of slender picks from his pocket, the boy kneeled down and began jiggling them in the lock.

"No need to destroy the poor guy's shop," he murmured.

"I see Arthur's been teaching you more than editing."

"Tools of the trade," Harry replied. "I am a journalist, after all."

There was a click, and the door swung open. Harry bowed to Raquella, and gestured for her to enter.

"Ladies first."

"You're too kind," the maid replied acidly, moving through into the shop. Harry winked at Jonathan behind her back.

"I think she likes me," he whispered out of the corner of his mouth.

"I'm not sure she does," Jonathan whispered back.

Harry frowned. "No. Maybe not."

The first thing that struck Jonathan upon entering Bartlemas Timepieces was the noise: the shop echoed with the insistent chirrup of ticking clocks, as though they were standing in a field of metal crickets. Every inch of space in the glass display cases and on the front counter was taken up with watches, hundreds of tiny mechanisms furiously working to keep pace with time. By the wall, a platoon of grandfather clocks stood stiffly to attention.

Unsure what he was looking for, Jonathan closed the front door behind him and begin to inspect the display cabinets. Suddenly there was an explosion of chimes and cymbals: Jonathan spun round, expecting to see some monstrous creature, while beside him Harry instantly adopted a fighting stance. Then, from the other side of the room, came the sound of Carnegie chuckling.

"Easy there, boys. Just the clocks. It's half past eleven."

Jonathan relaxed, feeling a little foolish.

Harry looked rueful. "It's been a while since I've done something like this – I think I'm out of practice."

"I'm not sure I've ever been *in* practice," Jonathan said. "I'm going to look upstairs."

He slipped behind the counter and headed up the stairs, pleased to leave the cacophonous ticking behind. He found himself in a high-ceilinged workshop, where rows of wounded watches spilled tiny cogs and coils out on to the workbenches. The centre of the room was dominated by a large upright piece of iron shaped like a fin. As the moonlight stole in through the windows, a shaft of white light bounced off the fin and arced out across the floor. Looking down at his feet, Jonathan saw that a clock face had been painted on to the floorboards.

There was the sound of footfalls on the stairs, and his companions appeared. Raquella passed her hand through the beam of moonlight.

"A moondial!" she breathed. "How wonderful."

"Not bad," Carnegie agreed. "But it doesn't tell us where Bartlemas is. Let's spread out."

Jonathan began a tour of the room, inspecting every broken watch in the hope of stumbling over some kind of clue. Near the window, he passed Harry, who was frowning, holding up a large sheet of paper boasting an immensely complicated diagram.

"What's that?" Jonathan asked.

"I'm not sure. I'm guessing it's some sort of clock."

"Looks more like a circuit board to me."

"A what board?"

"Never mind." Experience had taught Jonathan that Darksiders were best kept away from modern technology. He hadn't forgotten the first time Carnegie had encountered a television at Jonathan's house on Lightside – the wereman had growled suspiciously at the screen until it had been turned off.

Harry gathered up the plans and folded them into his back pocket.

"Anyone found anything?" he called out.

Carnegie shook his head. "There's nothing here."

"Not if you don't look properly," Raquella called out from underneath one of the workbenches. She emerged on her hands and knees, her black dress covered in dust. In her hand was a small calling card.

"One of the few advantages of being a maid," she said lightly, accepting the wereman's help up. "You know where things get lost."

The card read simply:

The Psychosis Club (Est'd. DY78)
Final Resting Place for the Lonely and the Forlorn
53A, The Grand

Jonathan had barely finished reading it when there came the sound of a carriage drawing up outside. Harry dashed to the window.

"We've got company," he reported.

Jonathan joined him at the window, and peered through the smeared glass to the street below. Although the carriage had stopped by the street lamp outside the front of the shop, steam rising from the flanks of the horses, no one got out.

"What are they waiting for?" asked Jonathan.

There came a deep rumbling sound by way of reply, and the pavement outside Bartlemas's shop began to shake.

"Uh oh," breathed Harry.

In a sudden eruption of stones and pebbles, two figures exploded from out of the pavement. They drew themselves up to their full height, necks slowly turning as they inspected their new surroundings.

Jonathan gasped. "Bow Street Runners!" he hissed.

"No kidding," Harry replied. "But what are they doing here?"

"More importantly," Carnegie growled softly, "who's in the carriage?"

The vehicle had maintained an aloof distance from the Runners, staying back in the shadows. Thick black drapes hung in the windows, and the side door was decorated with an ornate crest.

Carnegie let out a low whistle. "The plot thickens."

Jonathan was about to ask what he meant when the

door of the carriage opened and a man stepped out, his resplendent white hair shining in the streetlight.

"It's Holborn!" Harry exclaimed. "But why's the Abettor here?"

"We can find out later," Carnegie replied. "I don't like the look of this. Let's get out of here."

As he spoke, the Bow Street Runners stepped up to the wall of Bartlemas Timepieces and melted into the brickwork. The building trembled slightly, and then a series of heavy footfalls could be heard from downstairs.

"Come on!" the wereman hissed. He ran over to the side of the room and hauled open a window. Needing no second invitation, Harry swung out of the window and lithely scaled down the drainpipe to the ground below. Jonathan hadn't forgotten how athletic Harry was – but he was more surprised by Raquella, who quickly tucked up her skirt and clambered neatly after him.

There was a thud on the staircase. The Runners were coming.

Jonathan slipped quickly through the window and into the darkness, his breath frosting in the early winter air. Clinging to the pipe with cold fingers, he made his descent hand-over-hand, his feet struggling to get purchase on the brickwork. Near the bottom, the pipe wobbled violently, and Jonathan looked up to see that Carnegie had closed the window and followed after him. Realizing that the drainpipe wasn't strong enough to hold the both of them, Jonathan let go and dropped to the floor.

He found himself standing in a narrow alleyway that ran alongside Bartlemas Timepieces. At one end, the black carriage remained motionless at the pavement's edge. Harry and Raquella were already moving swiftly through the shadows in the opposite direction, into the bowels of the Lower Fleet. Jonathan was about to follow them when a movement caught his eye. It was Holborn. The Abettor had returned to the carriage, and was talking to someone in the back.

Carnegie landed easily on the ground beside him. "Time to go, boy," the wereman whispered, brushing his hands.

Jonathan pointed at the carriage. "Who's that with Holborn?"

"Who cares? If the Runners look out of the window, we're done for! Move!"

But just then Holborn opened the carriage door to climb inside. Before the wereman could drag him away, Jonathan caught a glimpse of another man huddled in the back seat of the Abettor's carriage.

He gasped.

It was Lucien.

11

By the time they reached the Grand it was well past midnight. Usually the riotous peak of Darkside's main street, the threat of the Bow Street Runners had somehow managed to quieten the savage menagerie. The pavements were unnaturally quiet, fists kept unclenched and insults swallowed. Doorways were unsullied by shadowy figures. Outside the Aurora Borealis candle shop, one foolhardy gang was taunting rivals across the street, hurling insults through the wheels of passing carriages; but whereas this would usually have been the prelude to a mass brawl, now they maintained a surly stalemate.

Trying his best not to look suspicious, Jonathan stuffed his hands in his pockets and walked nonchalantly alongside Carnegie. Having failed to persuade the teenagers to return to his lodgings while he visited the Psychosis Club alone, the wereman was lost in a moody silence. Jonathan knew that he was concerned about what they had seen outside Bartlemas's shop. Lucien was a large enough threat on his own – if he was now in league with the Abettor, the second most powerful figure in Darkside, there was no telling what he might be capable of. But if Carnegie was pensive, Harry was absolutely livid.

"You saw Holborn talking to *Lucien*?" he spluttered. "What's he thinking? It's the middle of the Blood Succession – the Abettor has to stay neutral!"

"It didn't look very neutral to me," Jonathan replied darkly.

"Bad news for Marianne," Carnegie added. "If Holborn's cosying up to Lucien, I'd say the odds on her winning the Succession aren't good."

"Even if Lucien and Holborn have joined forces," Raquella said slowly, "why are they bothering to chase after Bartlemas?"

"Good question," answered Carnegie. "I don't know. Something big is afoot here, and I've got a hunch your master's deeply involved in it."

Though the mood of his companions was downbeat, as Jonathan slipped through the subdued throng on the Grand, he had to confess to a feeling of strange elation. Lucien's return may have been bad news for Darkside, but it rekindled Jonathan's hopes that he could discover what had happened to his mum. All he had to do now was prise the truth from Lucien – admittedly, a task easier said than done.

The entrance to the Psychosis Club was notable for the large area of empty pavement outside, as though even those risking the Grand that night refused to walk past it. A hulking doorman in a formal black suit was standing guard by the arched front door, scanning the street with contempt. Two stunted, twisted horns rose out of his forehead. As Carnegie made to enter the club, the doorman placed a large hand across his chest.

"Where do you think you're going?"

"Inside."

"You know the rules, Carnegie. You can't come into the Psychosis Club unless you're on your own. And you *definitely* can't come in with a bunch of children."

"I know the rules, Pork," the wereman replied easily. "I'm just ignoring them."

"You don't want any trouble," the doorman said slowly, cracking his knuckles.

"Really?" Carnegie grinned wolfishly. "Who says?"

Pork hesitated, unnerved by the wereman's composure.

"Look," Carnegie said. "We just want to talk to someone. We'll be in and out in ten minutes. It's not worth a fight, however much fun that might be."

Pork scratched one of his horns, thinking hard. Eventually he moved to one side. "You've got five minutes," he said. "Then I'm coming looking for you."

Carnegie shrugged, then stepped past the doorman and through the archway. After sharing a dubious glance with one another, the three teenagers followed him.

The Psychosis Club was a dolorous honeycomb of low, vaulted caverns. At first glance, it appeared to be deserted, but as they walked onward they saw customers nursing drinks alone, their heads down, unwilling to make eye contact with anyone else. Droplets of water seeped through the ceiling on to the floor, trickling down the brickwork like tears.

From somewhere in the damp depths, there came the low sound of a fiddle. Jonathan followed the trail of the music into a slighter larger cavern, where a dishevelled, grey-haired man was playing on a semicircular stage, against a backdrop of blood-red drapes. He moved expressively, swaying in time to the music, his body rising and falling with every wailing note. Under the man's gentle touch, the fiddle sang a plaintive song of loss and heartbreak. Jonathan stood transfixed. He had never heard anything like it.

"Who is that?" he asked.

It was Raquella who replied – tears glistening on her cheek. "Isaac Lacrimoso. When he was a young man, a girl broke his heart, and he swore never to love anyone again. He's played here every night since. This song, nothing else."

As the notes soared higher and higher, the water began dripping faster through the ceiling, until it fell in a torrent that drenched everyone in the room. Jonathan could barely see Lacrimoso through the rain, but the wizened old man didn't seem to notice the downpour, utterly lost in a song he had played thousands upon thousands of times.

"It's so beautiful," Raquella breathed. "And so *sad*."

Lacrimoso drew his bow across the fiddle in a final, keening note. When the sound finally died, the deluge slackened as quickly as it had begun. His shoulders slumped, Lacrimoso shuffled off through the puddles on the stage and back through the red drapes to a silent ovation.

Jonathan was too shocked to clap. Instead, running a hand through his wet hair, he watched Carnegie stride over to the bar in the corner of the room, where a bored young man was staring off into space.

"What?" the barman asked in a surly tone.

"I'm looking for someone."

"Isn't everyone here?"

Carnegie reached over the bar and fastened his hand on the barman's shirt, pulling him so close that their noses were almost touching.

"Perhaps I didn't make myself clear," he said, through clenched teeth. "I'm looking for someone, and you're going to help me find him. We think he's a regular here – Josiah Bartlemas?"

"All right, guv," the barman said hastily, hands raised in the air. "The name rings a bell, but I couldn't say for sure. Honestly, most of the folks in here keep themselves to themselves. Isaac might know him, though." The barman pointed a trembling finger in the direction of the crestfallen fiddler, who now sat in a booth on his own. "He's in here every night. That's the best I can do, honest."

The wereman relented, removing his grip on the man's shirt claw by claw.

"See how easy that was?" he said brightly. "Thank you."

"You're . . . you're welcome," the barman stammered, before scurrying out of reach to the other side of the bar.

Raquella caught Carnegie's arm. "Let me talk to Lacrimoso," she said. "I don't think your usual tactics will work with him."

"My usual tactics work with everyone – eventually."

"Please?"

Carnegie nodded reluctantly. "Take the boy with you. Pierce – you can keep me company." The wereman slouched against the bar with Harry, while Jonathan followed Raquella over to the fiddler's booth.

The maid coughed, and said hesitantly: "Excuse me, sir?"

Isaac looked up and gazed at the maid with large, doleful eyes. He gasped.

"Can it be?" he breathed. "Maria?"

Raquella shook her head, her cheeks reddening. "No – my name is Raquella. I'm afraid I don't know who Maria is."

The fiddler inspected her closely, and saw Jonathan standing beside her. He sighed deeply. "Of course not. You must forgive an old fool – it's just, you have the same hair. Flowing red locks, like a field of roses. Please," he said, gesturing at the seat opposite, "sit down, both of you. Tell me what I can do for you."

"We're looking for a man called Josiah Bartlemas,"

Raquella began, as the two of them squeezed into the booth. "I was told you might know him?"

There was a pause, and then the fiddler nodded.

"Yes, I know Josiah. He comes in here every now and again. Sometimes we talk."

"When was the last time you saw him?"

Isaac frowned. "The night the Ripper died."

Jonathan leaned forward eagerly. "You saw him that night?"

"Yes – I remember because he was acting so strangely. Josiah was babbling that he had cracked some sort of code, and now a wheel could start turning. He was so excited that I couldn't make head nor tail of what he was saying. Then, when the Blackchapel Bell started ringing, an odd look came over his face. He put down his drink without a word and raced out. That was the last I saw of him."

"Did you know him well?" Raquella pressed.

"Josiah?" Isaac replied. "As well as the next man, I suppose. He was private, kept himself to himself. As far as I know, he didn't have any friends. He spent nearly all of his time in the shop. Watches and clocks were his passion, his obsession."

"Did he ever talk to you about his work?"

"Not really . . . I don't think he thought a mere fiddler could understand. From time to time Josiah boasted that he was involved with some sort of special project that was going to make him rich, but I didn't pay him much heed. I have heard many such stories in here before. . ."

As the fiddler smiled sadly to himself, Jonathan thought of the plans Harry had taken from Bartlemas's workshop. What if the watchmaker had been telling the truth – could they be the key to his secret project?

"Do you know where we could find him now?" he asked.

"If he's not in his shop, or here. . ." Isaac shrugged. "I've no idea."

The fiddler turned his sad eyes back to his drink, his voice trailing away. Thanking him quietly, Raquella and Jonathan got up and returned to the bar, where the sizeable figure of Pork had suddenly loomed up on Carnegie's shoulder. Producing a pocket watch, the doorman tapped it meaningfully with a thick finger.

"Time's up," he grunted.

"We were just leaving," Carnegie replied, favouring the doorman with a beatific smile. "Come on, Pork. I'll walk you out. We can fight another time."

As they climbed the steps out of the Psychosis Club and back on to the Grand, Jonathan felt a wave of tiredness wash over him. Having reached a dead end, all his energy had drained away, and he was suddenly desperate for bed. He hadn't slept since he had heard Vendetta was after him. How long had that been – two days?

They had to linger on the Grand in order to hail down carriages to take Raquella and Harry home, and the street lamps were burning low by the time Jonathan and Carnegie reached the wereman's lodgings. Carnegie unlocked the front door, yawning loudly, and began to climb the stairs. Jonathan was about to follow when a hand suddenly clamped down on his shoulder.

12

"Dad?" Jonathan's voice rang with astonishment.

It seemed unbelievable, but it was indeed Alain Starling standing in front of him. His dad was dressed in the Victorian style, sporting an open-necked white shirt, waistcoat and trousers beneath a black overcoat. The outfit was completed by a top hat set firmly on his head, and a stout walking stick that threatened to deliver a hefty clout. Although he looked surprisingly at ease in the perilous environment of Fitzwilliam Street, the beads of perspiration on Alain's forehead and the grey pallor to his skin hinted at the toll Darkside's atmosphere was taking on him. He was also, Jonathan couldn't help but notice, furious.

"What are you doing here?" said Jonathan. "You're not well enough for this!"

"What am I doing here?" Alain shot back. "I'm here to collect my son – who is in an *unbelievable* amount of trouble – and drag him back home. By his ears, if necessary."

"Oh, Dad—" Jonathan began.

"Don't 'oh Dad' me," Alain snapped. "You sneak out of the house in the middle of the night like a common thief, crossing over to Darkside when I *expressly* told you not to . . . the one time I forbid you to do something – with your safety in mind, to protect you – and you disobey me. You can't imagine how angry I am with you!"

At the sound of Alain's raised voice, Carnegie had stopped halfway up the stairs. Now he stalked back to the doorway, eyeballing Jonathan.

"Seems I owe you an apology, Alain," the wereman said. "The boy didn't tell me he'd gone behind your back. I would have hauled him back to Lightside myself if I'd known, Vendetta or not. Happy to do it now, if you want."

"Thanks, Elias, but I've got this one." Alain turned back towards his son. "Well? Anything to say for yourself?"

Jonathan thought for a second. "If I'd stayed, you'd have tried to protect me from Vendetta. Dad, he'd kill you! This was the safest thing for all of us. I'm sorry I didn't listen to you, and I'm sorry you've had to come here to find me, but don't make me go back." He looked up at Alain, eyes shining with excitement. "Lucien's come out of hiding! We don't know what he's up to, but it's something shady. Don't you see? Now he's out of hiding, we can make him tell us about Mum!"

"No doubt he'd be delighted to talk to you," Carnegie said sourly.

"He's all we've got," Jonathan retorted. "He's the only one who knows what happened." Turning back to Alain, he added softly: "And if you make me go home now, Dad, we might never get another chance to find out about Mum. That'll be it."

Before Jonathan's father could reply, Carnegie stepped between them, his eyes narrowing at the sight of a group of lads strutting down Fitzwilliam Street towards them.

"We'd better continue this upstairs," he growled. "That's a particularly nasty gang of troublemakers heading towards us, and I don't think this is the right time for a disagreement."

They headed smartly up to the wereman's lodgings, where Carnegie busied himself stirring up the fire in the hearth. Alain took off his hat and laid down his stick, before sinking into an armchair. As he rubbed his face wearily, he looked suddenly smaller and weaker than he had before. Jonathan stood and waited, unsure of what to do.

"I don't want to talk about this now," his dad said eventually. "It's late, and you look like you haven't slept for a week."

"Take the spare room," Carnegie said, stabbing at the coals with a poker. "You know the way."

Jonathan opened his mouth to argue, but took one look at his dad's face and closed it again. Back in the familiar surroundings of Carnegie's spare bedroom, he undressed quickly, convinced that there was too much churning round in his mind to sleep. Within seconds he was unconscious.

It was still light when he awoke, pale sunshine drifting in through the curtains. Down on Fitzwilliam Street, a shop owner was resignedly sweeping up the remnants of a shattered window. Despite the daylight, the air in the spare room was chilly, and Jonathan hopped barefoot across the wooden floor to slip on some trousers. He washed quickly in the hand basin, wincing at the feel of the icy-cold water on his skin.

The sound of Carnegie and his father talking was carrying in from the main room. Jonathan was about to join them when something about their urgent, hushed undertones made him pause at the door and listen.

"You went to Bartlemas's and you didn't tell him?" Alain said.

There was a pause.

"Didn't feel like the right time," Carnegie replied.

"Why on earth not? That shop was like a second home to me! He would have wanted to know!"

Suddenly, Jonathan realized why the name Bartlemas Timepieces had felt familiar. He had seen the shop before, in a photograph he had found in his dad's study. Alain and Theresa had been standing outside it, their arms around one another, looking young and happy and in love. His dad had worked there, and Carnegie had known about it, and he hadn't told him.

"Listen to me, Alain," Carnegie said carefully. "You haven't been here this past year. You haven't seen what Jonathan's been like."

"I think I know my own son."

"You don't understand!" the wereman said, his voice rising.

"Every time the boy finds out something new about either of you, he becomes convinced that he can find Theresa."

"And what is so wrong with thinking that?" Alain asked icily.

"For pity's sake, man!" Carnegie shouted. "It's been over ten years! She's dead!"

Time stopped. Jonathan caught his breath, frozen by the starkness of the wereman's words. Once more he was confronted by his greatest fear, a fear of such enormity that he was too scared to acknowledge it might be true. He barely heard the wereman continue more quietly: "Theresa's gone, Alain. She got tangled in something incredibly dangerous and paid the ultimate price. Ripper knows, I would give anything for that not to be the case, but you have to face up to the truth. Both of you. The longer you pretend otherwise, the more you're going to get hurt."

There was a long, painful silence, and then Alain said in a small voice, "I miss her so much, Elias."

"I know," Carnegie replied, with an unexpected softness. "I do too."

As the sound of his father crying floated in from the next room, Jonathan leaned his head against the door, unwilling to intrude on a private moment between the two men he loved most in the world, even as he felt the tears mist in his eyes and the world begin to flood around him.

Eight hours later, it was a sombre quartet who settled down to eat at The Last Supper, Darkside's most exclusive restaurant. Despite the fact that it normally took years of violence and skulduggery to get a table, and that the other clientele could barely contain their excitement as they smacked their lips and loosened their waistbands in anticipation, the atmosphere at Jonathan's table was subdued. The aromatic delights of the pickled eel left them unmoved, while even the spectacle of the immolated pigeon failed to lift the mood.

That afternoon, Jonathan had eventually emerged from his room pretending he had just awoken. He dutifully feigned surprise at the news that his dad had worked at Bartlemas Timepieces, and had agreed to accompany Alain and Carnegie on the long journey back to the shop. They arrived to find it a charred ruin. With the fires doused, the local residents had already forgotten about the building, passers-by barely bothering to glance at the devastation. As Jonathan and Carnegie looked on, Alain picked his way through the smouldering black timbers, distraught at the wreckages of watches and clocks littering the floor.

"All those years of work," he murmured to himself. "What a waste."

He had barely said a word since. Now he pushed a serving of devilled ostrich eggs around his plate, barely eating a mouthful. In stark contrast, Harry Pierce tucked hungrily into his food, one eye trained on Alain's leftovers. Posing as the new food critic of the *Informer*, Harry had managed to get them a table at the restaurant, and he appeared unwilling to miss the opportunity to try everything. Next to Harry, one seat on the pentagram-shaped table remained empty: Raquella had refused the invitation to dinner, citing duties at Vendetta Heights.

"Well, one thing's for sure," Jonathan said glumly. "If Holborn and Lucien were looking for Bartlemas, they didn't want anyone else picking up the trail."

"It doesn't make sense," Carnegie said. "Why go to all this trouble over a watchmaker?"

"Maybe it's not Bartlemas they're after," Harry said, swallowing a large mouthful of floured jellyfish. Dusting his hands clean, he removed a sheet of paper from his pocket and spread it out on the table. "Maybe it's this."

"Of course!" Jonathan exclaimed. "The plans!" With all the drama of the past twenty-four hours, he had nearly forgotten about them.

Alain looked up from his meal. "Plans?" he said curiously.

"Harry found them in Bartlemas's workshop. And this guy in the Psychosis Club said Bartlemas used to talk about some secret project he was working on. I think this might be it."

Instantly invigorated, Alain pushed away his plate and stood up. Pulling a small pair of spectacles from his pocket, he began poring over the plans.

"It's a clock, right?" asked Harry.

"Something like that, I'd guess," agreed Alain. "There's something very familiar about it."

Jonathan peered at the diagram over his dad's shoulder.

The mechanism was a square casing, within which three cogs with jagged teeth revolved around a tiny sphere. Bartlemas had labelled the diagram at the top of the page – Jonathan frowned as he tried to decipher the watchmaker's crabby handwriting.

"What's a . . . corset whelk?"

"Ah," Alain chuckled. "I should have known. It's not 'corset', son, it's Chronos. Chronos Wheel, in fact."

Jonathan's mind cast back to the Psychosis Club, and what Isaac Lacrimoso had said about the night Thomas Ripper had died: "*Josiah was babbling that he had cracked some sort of code, and now a wheel could start turning. . .*" Was this the wheel Bartlemas had been talking about?

"Whatever its flaming name," Carnegie butted in. "You know what it is?"

Alain nodded. "Only too well. And I know where we can find it."

"Where?"

"Greenwich. In Lightside." He gave Jonathan a challenging glance. "Still sure you don't want to go back?"

13

Later that night, on the other side of London, a small rowing boat was attempting to navigate the black, churning expanse of the Thames. A fierce wind had stung the river into life, large waves tossing the craft around as if it were driftwood. The rowing boat met its fate blindly: no lights signalled its presence or illuminated its path.

As another wave crashed over the edge of the boat, soaking Sergeant Charlie Wilson to the bone, the young policeman wondered for the hundredth time how he had managed to get himself in this mess. He was hunched in the stern, shivering as the boat lurched and rolled. Considering the conditions, it was a miracle they hadn't capsized – a feat due entirely to the hulking figure in the rowing seat, who was covered from head to toe in a cowled cloak. He battled the river with two giant oars that looked like tree trunks, the forelocks creaking and straining with the weight. The oarsman hadn't said a word from the minute Wilson had stepped uncertainly into the boat down by Southwark

Bridge. If he knew where they were going, or why their journey necessitated such an unusual method of transport, he wasn't going to share it.

Which was just typical these days, Wilson thought to himself sourly. From the moment he had agreed to join the mysterious Department D, the certainties of his previous life as a normal policeman had vanished. He had spent the past few months holed up in a windowless room in the depths of a London police station, rarely seeing his old friends and colleagues. There was no regular police work as such – Wilson hadn't visited any crime scenes, interviewed any suspects, or even gone out on patrol. Instead he whiled away the hours making notes on old military books analysing battles he had never heard of, and poring over maps of modern London. His only companions were a couple of sallow-faced old men and, of course, Detective Horace Carmichael.

Wilson's boss sat beside him in the stern of the boat, wrapped up in a blanket. He was staring out over the water, his mind elsewhere. An untidy, hunchbacked man, Carmichael was renowned as one of the sharpest coppers on the force, and one of the strangest. He spent his days reading newspapers, ignoring the high-profile crimes on the front page only to take interest in the most innocuous and ridiculous of stories. He never gave straight answers, preferring to talk in riddles – mumbling about how there were "two sides to every coin", and that "the truth was around the corner". If he was being honest, Wilson wasn't sure that Carmichael was entirely sane.

Despite the late hour, London was still alive: as they passed under Tower Bridge, Wilson could hear the rumble of traffic overhead. The rowing boat pitched violently over the crest of another wave, and Charlie looked back wistfully at the bright lights of the city and wished that he were anywhere but here. This was not the life he had imagined when he signed up to the force.

"Sir?" he shouted, above the roar of the waves.

Detective Carmichael shook his head, as though waking from a dream. "Yes – what is it?"

"I was just wondering, sir, now that we're on the water, whether you could tell me what we're actually doing?"

"Going to meet someone."

"In a rowing boat, sir?" Wilson spluttered, receiving another faceful of Thames water.

Carmichael looked away again, and then said, in a barely audible voice, "You've worked hard for me, Charlie. I appreciate that. Hopefully tonight will bring you the answers you're looking for."

A giant wave rose up in front of them like a wall of water, preventing Wilson from asking any further questions. Digging his oars into the river, the oarsman skilfully rode the wave, landing the boat safely on the other side with a mighty splash. He had been rowing for nearly half an hour without so much as a murmur. Despite everything, the sergeant couldn't help but marvel at the superhuman effort.

It had begun to rain, heavy drops pelting down upon the boat. The river bent to the left, winding round past

Rotherhithe and towards the Isle of Dogs. Behind Wilson, the centre of London was fading from view, the last lights on the riverbank winking out until they were only a memory. He felt his superior relax by his side.

"We're nearly there," Carmichael said. "Look."

Straining to see through the rain and the darkness, Wilson could just make out the squat outlines of the old dock warehouses on the right-hand side of the river. And then he saw it: beneath the warehouses, down at the waterline, a yawning archway carved into the brickwork. A Londoner from birth, Wilson had lost count of the number of times he had travelled up and down the Thames, but he had never seen anything like this before.

"What *is* that?" he gasped.

Carmichael smiled. "A gateway."

"But that's impossible . . . I would have known about it!"

"There's a lot about this city you don't know, Wilson," the hunchback replied. "As it happens, most of the time the archway is closed – you could pass it a thousand times and not know it's there. Tonight, however, we are expected."

Pulling on his left-hand oar, the oarsman began to navigate the boat through the waves towards the archway. As they passed through the entrance and were swallowed up in a tunnel of darkness, a shiver of foreboding ran down Wilson's spine. Although the water became calmer, the waves less ferocious, he found himself fighting an irrational urge to jump out of the boat. He felt suddenly sick, a tide of nausea rising up his throat. The ceiling crowded in over their heads – it was padded with a thick coating of green moss that made Wilson shudder every time it brushed the top of his head.

All in all, he was mightily relieved when they emerged from the tunnel into a small, circular pool surrounded on all sides by high stone walls. It was good to be able to see the sky again, even if it was scarred with curling wreaths of smoke, and the air soured by a foul odour. High above Wilson's head, a fog lamp had been placed on top of the wall, illuminating an iron ladder trailing down into the water. The oarsman manoeuvred towards the ladder, grunting for the first time as he tried to hold the vessel steady against the riverfront wall.

"Grab the ladder then, lad," Carmichael said sharply. "We haven't got all day."

Stung into action, Wilson reached over and took hold of the ladder. The boat was still rocking on the current, and the rungs were treacherously slippery, but he was a young, fit man, and he made quick work of the ascent. Clambering over the riverfront wall, Wilson sighed gratefully at the feel of solid ground beneath his feet. It was several seconds before he appraised his surroundings – what he saw took his breath away.

He was standing in the grounds of a building so vast that it made him dizzy to look up to the very top. With its extravagant confusion of gothic spires and arches, it possessed the grand beauty of a warped cathedral. But there was something else, a powerful atmosphere of dread that Wilson felt in his bones; as though each brick was stained with the blood of an awful crime. In front of him, a paved walkway led up to a side entrance in the building, gas lamps forming a solemn honour guard along the way.

Wilson stood staring, open-mouthed, until a loud rumbling sound behind him brought him to his senses. He turned to see Carmichael's hand appear on top of the riverfront wall. As the sergeant ran over and hauled the hunchback on to dry land, he was astonished to see that the rowboat was rocking emptily on the current. The oarsman had disappeared.

"Thanks," the detective panted. "I always have trouble with that bit."

"You've been here before?" Wilson said, a note of awe in his voice. "What on earth is this place, sir?"

"Blackchapel," Carmichael answered calmly. "The ancestral home of the Rippers."

"The Rippers? Who are they?"

The detective fixed Wilson with a serious look. "Listen to me. Tonight you're going to see and hear a lot of things you won't understand. In good time, everything will become clear, but it's imperative that for now you keep your questions to yourself. We're meeting a very important man, and one mistake could prove very costly indeed. Do you understand?"

Wilson nodded numbly.

"Good. Let's not keep him waiting, then."

Carmichael set off down the pathway towards the side

entrance, where Wilson now saw a figure waiting for them in the doorway. He was a large man with hair as white as snow who held himself with a stately assurance. Wilson was surprised to see him greet Carmichael with a warm, familiar handshake.

"Abettor Holborn," Carmichael said respectfully. "It's good to see you again."

The white-haired man nodded. "As with you, Horace. It has been quite some time."

"We have Thomas to thank for that. I was worried he was going to outlive us all."

"Alas, no," Holborn said, with a thin smile. "Thank Darkside. Please, come inside."

Without even glancing at Wilson, the Abettor turned and led them inside the building. They walked down a long, straight corridor, each wall boasting a giant mirror that ran along its entire length, before entering a small antechamber. It was lavishly decorated with plush armchairs, intricately carved furniture and a thick purple carpet that threatened to swallow up Wilson's feet.

As Carmichael and the sergeant settled into armchairs, Holborn walked over to a drinks cabinet and poured three measures of red wine into ornate silver glasses.

"I hope you will find this comfortable," he said, handing out the drinks. "I am afraid Lucien will not be joining us this evening. There has been a . . . complication regarding the Succession."

"Nothing I need worry about, I hope?" asked Carmichael.

"It is a trivial matter," Holborn replied, airily waving a hand. "It shall be resolved soon enough."

"It will need to be. We cannot delay the Blood Succession for long. You have made something of a gamble, aligning yourself with Lucien. Even if he wins, will Darkside accept him?"

The Abettor shrugged. "What choice will they have? Once he is crowned Ripper, the people will have to forget, or face the consequences."

"And of course," Carmichael added shrewdly, "there will be the reassuring presence of Thomas's faithful Abettor by Lucien's side. Always ready to take over should the need arise."

Holborn inclined his head. "Naturally. I live to serve the borough, after all."

Struggling to follow the conversation, Wilson lifted the silver goblet to his lips and took a sip of the thick red liquid.

Only to discover that it wasn't, in fact, wine.

Wilson cried out in shock, spitting the liquid on to the carpet. Holborn looked at him sharply.

"You'll have to forgive my companion's somewhat crude manners," Carmichael said, glaring at the young sergeant as he deliberately took a sip from his own goblet. "He hasn't been to Darkside before."

The Abettor cast an appraising eye over Wilson, who felt himself wilting beneath his inspection. His hands were trembling now. What kind of place was this?

"Can he be trusted?"

"I wouldn't have brought him if he couldn't," Carmichael replied levelly. "Wilson's been researching locations for the upcoming battle for us. If Lucien is going to fight Marianne in Lightside, we need to ensure that the odds are stacked in his favour. Thanks to Wilson, I think we've found the right place."

"Really?" Holborn said, his eyes lighting up. "Where?"

"Battersea Power Station, on the south side of the river. If we start preparing now – get our men in place, become familiar with the terrain – Marianne won't know what hit her."

Holborn raised a single white eyebrow. "We?"

"Department D will be present to make sure that things run smoothly," Carmichael said. "And that there is no . . . overspill out into the city. There is only so much I can cover up before people start to ask awkward questions. And, after all, it is my duty to ensure that the Darksiders don't cause too many problems in London proper."

"A duty for which Lucien shall reward you greatly."

"Let's just say that, like you, I have a vested interest in maintaining the status quo."

Holborn raised his glass of blood in a toast.

"To the status quo," he said, and drank deeply.

14

Raquella was down in the kitchen of Vendetta Heights when the phone began to ring.

Exhausted by the frenetic activity of the previous few days, she had woken late that morning, pulling on a dressing gown before padding out barefoot into the corridor. Normally in a house of such size, the servants' quarters would have been a hive of industry: solemn footmen hurrying to do their master's bidding, scolding the maids en route for gossiping as they folded bed linen and polished the silverware, while the rattle of pots and pans echoed up from the kitchens. Yet Raquella walked down through the house alone.

She knew that others couldn't fathom why she had chosen to stay in Vendetta's service. It was hard to blame them: after all, Raquella knew better than anyone the cold abyss that masqueraded as her master's soul. But the vampire and the maid had been living together for so long that he was all she knew. Vendetta's smallest human gestures – an amused smile, a brisk nod of appreciation, the biting back of an insult – carried the same weight as the most generous tribute or precious present. Although she would die before admitting it to another soul, the truth was Raquella didn't know what she would do without the vampire.

Down in the desolate kitchen, she lit the stove and heated up a saucepan of milk, gratefully warming her hands over the flame. Pouring the hot milk into a china cup, the maid had taken her first cautious sip when her ears caught the sound of a faint ringing noise.

The cup of milk fell to the floor, shattering.

Raquella raced up the stairs and out through the back door, the folds of her nightgown flapping around her ankles, and sped across the back terrace towards a circular white building dominated by large windows. The air was so cold it stung her cheeks, and the pebbles bit into her feet, but she barely noticed. Reaching the entrance, she yanked open the door and ran inside.

If Vendetta took pleasure in anything beyond money and death, it was his glasshouse. Finally rebuilt following a devastating explosion, it was more opulent than ever: a court of tropical flowers, resplendent in their bright blues, brilliant reds and violent yellows, dutifully attended by rows of heaters which raised the temperature until the atmosphere was thick with condensation. Although the first impression was one of delicate beauty, Raquella knew that there were dark secrets in the heart of the glasshouse:

poisonous plants, buried weapons, corpses rotting in the flower beds.

The maid hurried along the central pathway, splashing through the streams of water trickling across the flagstones, ducking to avoid the low-hanging vines. Feathery ferns brushed her arm as she went. On a patio table in the centre of the glasshouse, Raquella saw the source of the insistent ringing: Vendetta's telephone. Her master had spent a small fortune connecting the device to Lightside, creating an exclusive channel of communication that reputedly not even Blackchapel could match. Every call was a momentous occasion – if Raquella's hunch was right, perhaps never more so than now.

Finally reaching the phone, she snatched up the receiver and said, "Hello?"

And, over the crackling of the line, she heard a dry, familiar voice reply, "Hello, Raquella."

Her heart pounding, Raquella heard herself saying, "Master? Where have you been? I was worried."

Vendetta chuckled thickly. "No doubt. Circumstances dictated that I leave Darkside as quickly as possible. I'm afraid there wasn't the time for any emotional farewells."

"I am glad to hear that you are well, sir. Where are you?"

"My location is no concern of yours," the vampire replied curtly. "You never know who may be eavesdropping."

"Very good, sir." Raquella paused. "I . . . I found Mr Pelham. In the cellar."

Vendetta made a dismissive sound down the line. "Don't

shed any tears over the butler. Pelham got what he deserved. I caught him snooping around the cellar, and took the appropriate steps. It appears someone was paying him to keep an eye on me. Holborn, no doubt."

"The Abettor, sir? Why would he spy on you?"

"Holborn and I have never seen eye to eye. He always resented the influence I had over James Ripper. Has anyone from Blackchapel visited the Heights in my absence?"

"No, sir. . . But I did see Holborn outside the shop of Josiah Bartlemas. Lucien was with him."

If she was expecting a reaction from her master, she was to be disappointed.

"Yes," Vendetta said, "I suspected that might turn out to be the case. It makes my task here only more pressing." There was a pause. "What were you doing at Bartlemas's shop?"

Raquella silently cursed her slip. "I was looking for a watch for my father, sir," she lied. "It is his birthday soon."

There was a long pause. "Raquella, it is fair to say that you have not always displayed the loyalty one would expect from household staff. I left Darkside in search of your friend Starling, but he disappeared before I could get to him. Almost as though someone had warned him."

Her heart sinking with dismay, the maid stayed silent.

"Luckily, I found someone else who met my . . . requirements. Even so, Raquella, there is only so much disloyalty I can allow."

"Yes, sir."

"We will discuss it further on my return," the vampire intoned coldly. "In the meantime, stay away from Bartlemas."

"When should I expect you home, sir?"

"If all goes well, after the Blood Succession. You will know if I have been successful."

"Good luck, sir."

"Oh, and Raquella?"

"Yes?"

"If I'm right, Holborn will do anything in his power to prevent me from achieving my goal. The Heights are far from safe at present. Watch your step."

There was a click, and the line went dead.

Raquella placed the receiver back in its cradle, troubled by the vampire's final warning. She left the glasshouse slowly, checking the wide expanses of the grounds for movement. As usual, there was no sign of life among the bare oaks that lined the estate, or in the dark hedgerows that formed the maze. Raquella felt suddenly, keenly alone.

Locking the back door behind her, the maid returned to the kitchen and began mopping up the spilled milk. She was sweeping up the shards of china when she heard the unmistakable sound of footsteps coming from the room above her head.

Raquella froze. As the footsteps padded stealthily around the ground floor, a voice in her head told her to run out of the back door and out through the grounds. But for some reason she stayed where she was. With Vendetta away, Raquella was the mistress of the household – and there was no way she was going to allow an intruder to have the run of the building.

Taking a deep breath, Raquella warily ascended the stairs to the ground floor. The footsteps had stopped, replaced by a persistent tapping noise that came from beyond the dining-room door. Pausing only to select an umbrella from the stand as a makeshift weapon, Raquella crept towards the dining room, and pushed the door open.

Inside, a boy was sitting in Vendetta's chair at the head of the long dining table, absent-mindedly drumming on the wooden surface with two large ebony-handled spoons. It was Harry.

"You!" Raquella shouted, startling Harry into dropping one of the spoons. "What on Darkside are you doing in here? You frightened me half to death."

"Sorry," he replied casually, not looking in the least bit penitent. "I knocked, but no one answered."

"That's not an invitation for you to break in!" Raquella said indignantly, laying the umbrella down on the table.

"I was worried!"

Even though the words sounded sincere, there was a smile playing on Harry's lips. He really was an exasperating boy, far too sure of himself. Raquella could never shake the impression that secretly he was poking fun at her – a fact that riled the maid beyond belief. And unlike Jonathan, Harry seemed impervious to her sharp tongue.

"Your chivalry is touching," she said coldly. "But as you can see, I am fine. Feel free to leave the same way you came in."

"What I'm trying to work out," Harry said thoughtfully, ignoring her, "is what could be so important that it would make you go outside half-dressed on one of the coldest days of the year."

Suddenly aware that she was still in her bedclothes, Raquella drew her dressing gown around her. The colour was rising in her cheeks – from anger, she told herself, not embarrassment.

"You'll have to forgive me. If I'd been expecting burglars, I would have dressed appropriately."

Harry made a placatory gesture. "OK, I'm sorry. Look, there was another reason I came here – Jonathan's going back to Lightside to look for Bartlemas. I thought you might want to join us."

Raquella shook her head. "I'm in enough trouble as it is. My master suspects me of helping Jonathan."

"You've spoken to Vendetta?"

The maid nodded. "He is already angry with me – if he finds out that I have been searching for Bartlemas, then I have no hope. I have done all I can. Jonathan is with Carnegie, and far away from Vendetta's grasp. What happens to him now is out of my hands."

"And what's going to happen to you?" asked Harry. He was no longer smiling.

"Why do you care?"

"Jonathan's got Carnegie and his dad to look out for him. Only fair that someone's looking out for you, too."

Raquella searched Harry's face for traces of mockery, but this time she couldn't find any. Was he actually being serious?

"This would be so much easier if you weren't quite so annoying," she said finally.

"I might be less annoying if you weren't quite so prickly."

There was a pause, and then they both smiled.

"I'll do you a deal," Harry said. "Tell me what Vendetta said to you, and I'll promise not to annoy you for the rest of the day."

"That seems like a reasonable trade," Raquella relented. "First of all, though, I'd like to get dressed."

She left the room, choosing to ignore Harry's impudent grin. Really, she fumed to herself as she ascended the staircase leading to her bedroom, the boy had the manners of a guttersnipe. The Ripper lineage was not what it used to be.

There was a creak on the stairs behind her.

"Harry, enough!" she shouted, whirling round.

The creature facing her wasn't Harry. Although it was dressed in normal Darkside clothes – jerkin, trousers and a cloth cap – its mottled skin was green and blistered with pustules. It was a hobgoblin. Raquella had seen her master deal with such creatures before: they were loathsome, unscrupulous beasts, hired for tasks more self-respecting Darksiders would eschew. This one smelled worse than any she had seen before. It was also carrying a long-bladed knife.

Twisting its face into a leer of pleasure, the hobgoblin took a menacing step towards the maid.

"Help!" she screamed.

As she backed away from the creature, Raquella heard the sound of running feet. Harry came skidding round the corner, athletically flipped himself over the balustrade, and bounded up the stairs towards the hobgoblin. The maid noticed that he was still clutching one of the ebony-handled spoons in his hand.

Snarling with annoyance, the hobgoblin turned and slashed wickedly at Harry with the knife. In a single flowing movement, the boy ducked out of harm's way and rapped the creature on the kneecap with the heavy spoon. There was an audible crack of metal on bone – the hobgoblin shrieked in pain. Following up, Harry grabbed the creature by the collar and used its own momentum to send it stumbling over the balustrade. There was a wail of horror as the hobgoblin started to fall, and then a sickening thump as it hit the floor ten feet below. It had been over in a matter of seconds.

Raquella sagged down on the steps with relief. Harry tossed the battered spoon over the side of the staircase and sat down beside her, breathing heavily.

"A *spoon*?" she said eventually.

"You sounded like you were in trouble," Harry replied defensively. "I didn't have time to swap it for anything better."

The maid peered over the balustrade at the crumpled form of the hobgoblin.

"You seemed to manage," she conceded.

"Let me help you, and I'll show you what I can do with a fork." Harry winked. "It's really quite impressive."

Raquella shook her head, but allowed Harry to help her to her feet. It appeared she wasn't going to be left on her own, after all.

15

The Docklands Light Railway train moved sinuously through the grey London morning, following a winding path around the skyscrapers of Canary Wharf. Every change of points, every stop and start was computerized; there were no drivers on the DLR. They were ghost trains. In his seat at the front of the lead carriage, Jonathan watched through drizzle-splattered windows as the track unfolded out in front of him. He was used to tube trains charging blindly through the Underground – this felt as though he were at the controls of some sort of giant computer game.

Jonathan nudged his dad and pointed ahead.

"We're nearly there," he said. "That's Greenwich."

Alain didn't reply, merely shifting uncomfortably in his seat. He had been quiet all morning. They had risen early, taking a carriage across Darkside to Rookwood Maps and Globes, a cluttered shop whose enterprising owner, Carmen, charged people for use of the crossing point that ran beneath the floor. Carnegie had reluctantly handed over several coins before leading them down the passageway that came out on a dirty side alley off Oxford Street. Although his dad hadn't said anything, Jonathan had seen his grimace of pain as they stepped over the boundary, and knew that Darkside's poisonous atmosphere had taken its toll on him. The years he had spent in the rotten borough had permanently damaged Alain's health – without Darkside blood in his veins, Jonathan wasn't sure how many more crossings his dad could take.

Back in modern London, the electronic cacophony of the city jarring Jonathan's ears, they hastened down the Central Line from Oxford Circus to Bank, where they had caught the DLR. The change in atmosphere didn't appear to have helped Alain – even now, his forehead glistened with sweat, and his jawline was taut with tension.

"Are you all right?" Jonathan asked.

His dad nodded. "Fine," he replied tersely. "How's Elias?"

Jonathan looked behind them to see the wereman lazily picking at his teeth with a long fingernail, oblivious to the discomfort of the businessman hemmed in next to him. With his battered suit and bewhiskered cheeks, Carnegie looked like a cross between an eccentric artist and a down-and-out.

"Looks OK to me," Jonathan reported. "As long as he's not on a bus, he's fine. Are you sure we're going to the right place?"

"If we're talking about the Josiah Bartlemas I knew, we'll find him at the Greenwich Observatory. Remember the name we saw on the plans Harry found?"

Jonathan's brow furrowed. "The Chronos Wheel?"

"Right. Well, that was the most famous invention of Wilbur Bartlemas, who just happened to be Josiah's grandfather. Wilbur was the Astronomer Royal at the observatory a hundred years ago, and was renowned for his inventions to do with watches and timekeeping."

"What was so special about the Chronos Wheel, then?"

Alain laughed. "It didn't work."

"Eh?"

"More than that, no one had any idea what it was *supposed* to do. Wilbur refused to demonstrate it to anyone. Not even Josiah knew how it worked, though he spent years trying to work it out. He was born in Greenwich, you know."

"Bartlemas is a Lightsider?" Jonathan said with surprise.

"Half-Lightsider – like all the best people." Alain's face broke into a smile, and gave his son a friendly nudge. "When we used to work in the shop together we'd stay up all night talking about London. Josiah loved to hear about the city, how it had changed since he had left. Technology fascinated him. I'd bring back digital watches and watch him take them apart. He always said they wouldn't catch on in Darkside, but secretly I think he was quite taken with them. Speaking of time – what is it now?"

Jonathan delved into his jeans pocket and took out his

Darkside pocket watch. He found its chunky weight in his pocket reassuring, whereas he had never felt comfortable with a mobile phone or with a modern watch strapped around his wrist.

"Just gone midday," he said.

"We've got an hour to get to the observatory," Alain said. "I've got a feeling he'll make his move at one—" He gave a sharp intake of breath, and clutched at his side.

"Dad!" Jonathan said. "What's wrong?"

"It's all right, son," Alain replied, through clenched teeth. "It's just the crossings. . . I'm not as strong as I used to be. . ."

Suddenly Carnegie was crouched by their side. "Problem?"

"It's Dad – he's not well."

Carnegie cast a critical eye over Alain. "You look done in," he said. "You need to rest up. Once we get to this Greenwich place, you're taking a cab home."

"But what about Josiah?" Alain protested. "If you're going to try and find him, you'll need me there. You don't even know what he looks like!"

"He's a Darksider. I'm sure we'll manage to pick him out. With you in this state, you'd be more of a hindrance than a help."

"I'm sick of this!" Alain snapped suddenly. "I feel so *useless*!"

"You'll be even less use if you kill yourself," the wereman said bluntly. "What if we need you then?"

Jonathan's dad looked like he was going to argue, but another sharp pain in his side stalled him. Eventually he nodded weakly, and allowed himself to be manoeuvred off the train at Greenwich, up the escalators and out on to the high street. Even though the rain was coming down harder now, and there was an icy chill to the air, the gentle, winding streets were busy with shoppers.

As he scanned the road for a taxi, Carnegie snarled suddenly. "I don't believe this!"

"What is it?" said Jonathan.

He jerked his head back towards the train station. "We've got company."

Following his gaze, Jonathan's heart sank. There, above a sea of heads, was the unmistakable face of Humble, Marianne's giant mute henchman. He was leaning against the station entrance, a foot taller than anyone else in the crowd, an enigmatic smile on his face. His feral partner Skeet was bounding up and down at his side with giddy menace.

"What are *they* doing here?" Jonathan asked incredulously.

"I doubt it's to give us a hand. Come on."

Throwing a supporting arm around Alain, Carnegie ushered them down the high street, muttering oaths under his breath. Humble and Skeet strolled nonchalantly after them – neither appeared to be in a hurry. As they rounded the corner and passed out of sight, Alain stumbled, and had to be helped upright by Carnegie. Jonathan's dad looked dead on his feet. Sizing up their options, the wereman glanced across the street, his eyes alighting upon a passageway beneath the sign "Greenwich Market".

"I can't look after both of you," Carnegie said. "Jonathan, you go in there and keep your head down. I'll make sure Humble and Skeet follow me, and then I'll get Alain into a cab. Stay put, and I'll come and find you."

"But what about Dad?"

"I'll make sure he's safe. Move, boy!"

With a final glance back at his dad, Jonathan jogged across the road and down the passageway. He came out in a genteel covered market, the rain drumming on a corrugated roof that slanted down over his head. The narrow aisles between the stalls were filled with shoppers hunting for early Christmas presents, the air thick with good-natured haggling and the warm smell of scented candles and coffee beans.

Preoccupied by concern for his dad, Jonathan wandered among the stalls, barely noticing the strange jumble of items for sale: rare books and flowing dresses; old-fashioned board games and intricate silver jewellery. After about ten minutes of aimless meandering, he found himself standing in front of a stall selling handcrafted children's toys. The stallholder, a shifty-looking young man, watched suspiciously as Jonathan idly picked up a carved wooden box bearing the inscription "Jack-In-The-Box". He flicked the lid open, but instead of a clown, a cloaked figure brandishing a tiny knife sprang forth. As it bobbed on its spring, the knife came down again and again on its imaginary victims. Jonathan shuddered. Whoever had designed the thing had a sick sense of humour. He turned over the box and searched the base for a maker's mark. When he found it, everything made a lot more sense:

Disraeli Toys & Amusements
14, The Grand

It seemed as though traces of Darkside were everywhere these days. Jonathan looked up to question the stallholder, but the man had vanished. He put down the jack-in-the-box and made to move away.

"Boo!" a voice said lightly in his ear.

He jumped, and then immediately cursed himself. This he should have expected. Summoning all his self-control, Jonathan turned round slowly and said, as evenly as he could manage:

"Hello, Marianne."

The Ripper heir and bounty hunter was standing beside him, inspecting one of the jack-in-the-boxes. Her dyed pink hair had been cut into a bob, held in place with a single black hair clip. By contrast, her alabaster skin was so pale it was almost colourless. There was the faintest smell of her special perfume in the air, which – Jonathan knew from experience – in larger doses could confuse and distract those around her. At his greeting, she put down the toy and graced him with a smile.

"Hello, Jonathan. Miss me?"

Which was a difficult question to answer. Jonathan seemed to have spent most of his time in Darkside fighting Marianne in one way or another. She had placed both him and his dad in mortal peril. And yet, maddeningly, he wasn't entirely unhappy to see her. Not that he was going to admit it.

"Not really. Why are you here?"

"What can I say?" Marianne waved an airy hand around the market. "I'm a sucker for a bargain."

"Looks like Humble and Skeet are too. I saw them outside."

"Yes – I asked them to divert that tiresome mongrel you're always with."

"If they touch either Carnegie or my dad, they'll regret it," Jonathan said fiercely.

"Oh, don't be so melodramatic," Marianne drawled. "I said 'divert', not 'maim'. No one's going to get hurt. I just thought it might be easier to talk to you if we were alone."

"Well, here we are. Why do you want to talk to me?"

"You asked me what I was doing here. I've crossed over because a contact of mine has informed me that a foolish watchmaker is meddling in affairs that really don't concern him. Given the circumstances, I can't afford to let this happen. The more important question, Jonathan, is what on Darkside are *you* doing here?"

"Just browsing," Jonathan replied flippantly. "I like a bargain too, you know."

Marianne's hand snaked out and seized him by the elbow.

"Is this a game to you?" she said, her voice now as cold and hard as a blade. "This is the Blood Succession we're talking about. Within days either my brother or I will be dead. And I can promise you this, Jonathan: meddle in the Rippers' affairs and you will be too. It might even be me that has to kill you, which would be a shame. I've grown rather fond of you."

"You've got a funny way of showing it," Jonathan said ruefully.

A shadow passed across Marianne's face, and suddenly she looked younger than before. Her grip softened.

"I am a Ripper, Jonathan. Darkness runs through my veins. There is only so much I can control – only so much I want to control. Can you understand that? I came to you to warn you: leave this place now, and leave the Blood Succession alone. I will not be so gentle again. And you would do well to remember one thing: if I'm here, then my brother will be too."

Jonathan suppressed a shiver. Instinctively, he looked around him, half-expecting to see Lucien's dark, haunted face among the jovial crowds. Instead, he was comforted by the sight of an irate wereman pushing towards him.

"Carnegie's back," Jonathan said, emboldened. "Do you want to warn him, too?"

There was a second, before she regained her usual demeanour of idle amusement, when Jonathan could have sworn there was a look of sadness on Marianne's face. Only for a second, though.

"Regrettably, I have to be somewhere," she said lightly. "Better be going. Wouldn't want to be late."

And with a flick of brilliant pink hair, the bounty hunter melted into the crowd and was gone.

16

The observatory had been built on top of the highest hill in Greenwich Park, secreted away behind a screen of thick evergreen trees. As Jonathan passed through the park gates, he could just make out the tips of the observatory's turrets poking out above the treeline, one bearing a giant red ball skewed on what looked like a crazed weathervane. His pulse quickened in anticipation. Although Jonathan had no idea what lay in store, he couldn't shake the feeling that his dad had been right, and that somewhere at the hill's summit, Josiah Bartlemas was waiting for them.

He checked his pocket watch again.

"It's quarter to one," he told Carnegie. "We'd better get a move on."

The wereman rolled his eyes. "I don't suppose your dad actually told us *why* we had to be there for one o'clock?"

"Not really. But it looks like Marianne's going to be there too, and I'd rather we got there first."

"Guess we'd better hurry up, then. Lead the way, boy."

In a city that throbbed to the rhythm of its seven million citizens hurrying from one place to another, Greenwich Park provided a welcome change of pace. A series of leisurely, undulating commons interspersed with snaking pathways, during high summer the park became a patchwork of picnic blankets and bouncing footballs, as Londoners flocked to escape the heat-trapped streets. Even in late November, with the grass soaked by drizzle, there were still people out cycling and walking dogs. A group of tourists were labouring up the steep hill towards the observatory, weighed down by guidebooks and digital cameras. Jonathan and Carnegie hurried past them, ignoring the stares that the wereman's appearance invited. As they climbed, a landscape of rooftops and tower blocks loomed up through the rain, dominated by the trinity of skyscrapers stretching up into the air on Canary Wharf.

The path levelled out at the entrance to the observatory, next to a broad avenue that ran along the crest of the hill. Aware that he had no Lightside money in his pockets, Jonathan was relieved to see that admission inside the building was free. Two smartly dressed attendants stood in the doorway, greeting tourists as they entered.

"I'll go first, boy," Carnegie said briskly. "No telling what's going to happen when we get in there."

"It's only an observatory, Carnegie – how much trouble can there be?"

"If your track record is anything to go by, more than enough to go round. Stay behind me."

The wereman swept through the entrance and into a large wood-panelled room filled with glass cases displaying old watch mechanisms and navigational devices. Jonathan inspected the labels, looking for the Chronos Wheel, but it was nowhere to be seen. They moved on, out into a cobbled courtyard surrounded by the low buildings that made up the observatory and the old house of the Astronomer Royal. An iron railing marked the place where the ground suddenly fell away, providing visitors with a sweeping view of London. A man was feeding coins into a mounted telescope, taking in the panoramic view of the city.

To Jonathan's right, a straight metal line had been sunk into the cobbles, marking the path of the Meridian Line, which signalled the meeting point of the eastern and western hemispheres. A gaggle of dispirited French schoolchildren were standing under the trees next to the line, attempting to shelter from the rain. In another corner of the courtyard, a lady dressed in Victorian costume was giving a talk to a group of tourists. They craned their necks as she pointed up at the roof of the observatory, towards the large red sphere Jonathan had seen from the park gates.

"This," the guide proclaimed, in a loud, theatrical voice, "is our famous time ball. At precisely one o'clock every day, the ball drops to the bottom of the pole. You can set your watches by it!"

Jonathan nudged Carnegie. "Did you hear that? One o'clock!"

"It would make sense," the wereman admitted. "If Bartlemas is trying to get his hands on the Chronos Wheel, he could do with a distraction. Maybe that'd do the trick."

Jonathan looked up at a signpost pointing out the different attractions and exhibitions. He scratched his head.

"The Chronos Wheel could be anywhere. Where do we look now?"

Before Carnegie could reply, there was a flash of pink hair at the entrance to the courtyard, and Marianne strolled into view. She was arm-in-arm with Humble, a guidebook clutched in her hand, glancing about her with the interested air of a tourist. Skeet trailed behind them, jabbering to himself disconsolately as he punched a fist into his palm.

"Think it's too late for treasure-hunting, boy," Carnegie said. "We're in the right place. Let's stay here and see what happens."

As the clock ticked closer to one, the courtyard swelled with tourists. The air was filled with the click and whirr of cameras, and a sense of vague anticipation. Even the French schoolchildren had come out from under the trees and were looking up expectantly at the time ball, hoping that the spectacle would make up for the rest of the day's disappointments.

Jonathan stood on his tiptoes and peered through the crowd, hoping to catch a glimpse of something out of the ordinary – strange clothing or the glint of a weapon – any hint that a Darksider was present.

"Bartlemas should be here by now!" Jonathan exclaimed. "Where is he?"

"He'll show his face soon enough," the wereman replied coolly. "What I want to know is: where's Lucien?"

There was a loud pop, and a flash of light from the other side of the courtyard. Jonathan whirled round, but it was only Humble, who had produced an old-fashioned camera and was photographing Marianne as she straddled the Meridian Line. The French children giggled, as if the giant and the lady with the dyed hair were merely other eccentric guides. Carnegie shook his head.

"That woman and her blasted games. She just doesn't know when to stop."

The wereman continued muttering away, but Jonathan was no longer listening. The hairs on the back of his neck were prickling, and he had the feeling that something was terribly wrong. As he looked back towards the iron railing, he saw that the man using the telescope had spun it the wrong way round, so that it was facing back into the courtyard. And he had trained it directly on Jonathan.

For a couple of seconds neither of them moved, until the man stepped out from behind the telescope and awkwardly down into the crowd, favouring one leg over the other. Before he vanished into the throng, he gave Jonathan a lingering glance, presenting a sallow face haunted by cruelty.

Jonathan's blood froze. He grabbed Carnegie's arm.

"Lucien!" he breathed.

"Where?" rapped the wereman.

"I lost him. He was by the telescope. I swear it, Carnegie, he's here!"

There was a ripple of excitement in the crowd, and then the French children suddenly began to count down from ten:

"*Dix! Neuf!*"

His heart pounding, Jonathan frantically scanned the sea of faces for Lucien. Where had he gone?

"*Huit! Sept!*"

By the Meridian Line, Humble put down his camera and moved to the back of the crowd.

"*Six! Cinq!*"

A low growl emanated from Carnegie's throat, his long fingers twitching hungrily.

"*Quatre! Trois!*"

Marianne reached inside her trench coat, revealing the hilt of a weapon.

"*Deux!*"

The bounty hunter smiled: a thin, cold challenge.

"*Un!*"

The time ball dropped down the pole, to a chorus of cheers and applause. At the same time, there came the sound of breaking glass from inside the building beneath it, and a scream. A spindly man with a hooked nose came scurrying out through the doorway and down the steps, a small wooden box underneath his arm.

"Bartlemas!" Jonathan cried.

At the sound of his name, the old man faltered. He glanced over towards them with wide, fearful eyes, and then broke into a scuttling run towards the exit – a doorway leading back through the observatory. With a snarl, Carnegie began pushing his way after the watchmaker, but Jonathan could see that he wouldn't get there in time. With his long stride, Humble had eased around the back of the crowd and was now standing in front of the exit, blocking off Bartlemas's escape route. As the giant took a menacing step towards him, the watchmaker drew a small pistol from his belt with a trembling hand and fired off a shot.

"Humble!" Marianne shouted.

At the sound of the gunshot, the tourists scattered like leaves. Through a blizzard of screaming children, Jonathan saw Marianne battling her way towards the giant mute, a large axe grasped in her left hand. Humble was still standing, disbelief on his face as he looked at the bullet in the door frame beside him, only inches from his head. In front of him, the watchmaker remained rooted to the spot, shaking with fright.

Jonathan watched as Carnegie neared Humble, unaware that Marianne's other henchman was bounding up behind him. Without thinking, Jonathan raced across the courtyard and threw himself into Skeet, in a rugby tackle that sent the pair of them crashing to the wet cobblestones. Jonathan felt a sharp pain course up his right elbow. Clenching his teeth, he hung on for dear life as Skeet howled and thrashed his legs, trying to break free. The creature twisted suddenly and caught Jonathan with a kick in the ribs, causing the boy to roll away in pain.

As he clutched at his side, Jonathan heard a bellowing roar echo around the courtyard. Carnegie was bent double, his body shaking violently as his muscles spasmed and his veins bulged. When the wereman looked up again, his face was matted with hair, and his eyes were pitiless black holes. The beast stalked towards the quivering Bartlemas, swatting the pistol from his hand and dragging the watchmaker away from Humble. The mute looked on thoughtfully, apparently unsure whether or not to tackle the beast on his own.

A stillness had descended on the courtyard. There were only the six of them left now, although the sound of crying schoolchildren could still be heard on the breeze. There was no sign of Lucien anywhere. With Marianne and her henchmen blocking the exit, Carnegie retreated towards the iron railing, his jaws snapping threateningly in their direction. The wereman's arm was locked around Bartlemas's neck, as though he was taking the watchmaker hostage. Bartlemas was whimpering softly, his hands still clutching the wooden box.

Jonathan picked himself up and moved cautiously alongside Carnegie. The beast dismissed him with one feral glance, and turned his attention back towards their assailants. Side by side, they backed away, as Marianne and her henchmen closed in on them. Wiping a damp strand of pink hair away from her cheek, the bounty hunter pointed at Bartlemas with her axe.

"I warned you, Jonathan," she called out. "Give me the watchmaker, or you'll die right here."

Before he could reply, there was a ghastly, inhuman screech, and then the world went black.

17

It was as though some evil power had doused the sun. Jonathan was suddenly and shockingly blind. The darkness was absolute: he could no longer make out the observatory buildings, nor the London skyline, or even the figures standing around him.

Yet far worse than the blindness was the fear. As the unnatural night fell, a coldness struck at the very marrow of Jonathan's bones. He suddenly felt helplessly young and alone, as if he were the only person on the planet. As the smell of decayed flesh infected his nostrils, Jonathan knew that Lucien had trapped them. The Ripper could transform himself into the Black Phoenix, a vicious bird of prey that hunted under a cloak of darkness. Jonathan and Carnegie had fought the Phoenix before – that they were still alive at all was due to a combination of luck and Marianne's intervention. They couldn't hope to be so fortunate again.

As Jonathan stood there, gulping with terror, sounds

reached him through the blackness: the choked cries of the watchmaker; a mournful howl – whether from Carnegie or Skeet, he couldn't be sure; from somewhere overhead, the beating of leathery wings, and a chill screech of triumph as the Phoenix swooped down towards them; and then, finally, a woman's shrill battle cry.

The inky cloud parted, and Jonathan caught sight of a shock of pink hair and the gleam of a blade as it traced a slicing arc through the air. Then the Phoenix was upon Marianne, in a maelstrom of fetid black feathers and razor-sharp talons. The bounty hunter rolled to one side as the bird's claws scraped against the cobblestones, before drawing a dagger from her boot and hurling it at the shadow. The Phoenix let out an ear-splitting screech of pain, and the cloud wavered once more. As Jonathan felt the fear within him ebb, he looked up to see Carnegie thrusting Bartlemas towards him.

"Get him out of here," the wereman growled, flexing his claws. "We'll take care of things up here."

Jonathan didn't want to leave Carnegie to fight the Phoenix, but it was pointless – not to mention dangerous – to protest. He bit back an objection and scanned the observatory for a way out. The Black Phoenix was hovering above the main exit, confronted by the combined force of Carnegie, Marianne, Humble and Skeet. Any attempt to run in that direction would end in disaster. Instead, Jonathan turned and looked out over the iron railing. It was a long drop down on to a steep incline dotted with trees.

Bartlemas followed his gaze. "Are you mad? The fall will kill us!"

Jonathan didn't bother to argue – he simply grabbed the spindly watchmaker and bundled him unceremoniously over the barrier. Within a second, he had leapt after him.

The pair of them hit the ground with a thump and went tumbling down the slope, bouncing painfully through the dirt, roots and branches tearing at their clothes, until a tree trunk brought Jonathan's progress to an abrupt halt. As he lay there, stunned, the sounds of battle floated down from the observatory: howls and screeches, blades ringing against talons.

And then Marianne's voice, crying, "Jonathan! He's coming for you!"

Darkness was sweeping down the hillside towards them like a black avalanche. Jonathan staggered over to where Bartlemas was crouching on his haunches.

"We've got to run!" he urged. "Come on!"

The watchmaker took one look at the cloud pursuing them and began haring down the hill. He proved a surprisingly quick runner, his long, skinny legs eating up the ground. Jonathan followed in his wake, his limbs battered and bruised, spurred on by the shadow on his shoulder, and the knowledge that the Phoenix was gaining on them.

At the bottom of the hill, the park levelled out, and the running became easier, even though the grass was still slippery with rain. There was a screech behind them, terribly loud in Jonathan's ears. The main exit was far away in the left-hand corner of the park; they would be dead before they reached it.

In front of them, a low stone wall separated the park from the National Maritime Museum, a series of graceful white buildings linked by a broad colonnaded walkway. Overtaking Bartlemas, Jonathan cried, "Follow me!" and raced towards the museum.

He placed a hand on the low wall and vaulted over the top of it in one smooth motion. As he turned to help Bartlemas, he saw that the Phoenix hovered over them, close enough for Jonathan to see the bird's bloodstained beak arrowing hungrily towards the watchmaker. Bartlemas was stuck with one leg on either side of the wall – Jonathan pulled him over, so hard that the pair of them fell to the ground. The Phoenix's talons passed centimetres over their heads, and the thick smell of rotting meat once again turned Jonathan's stomach.

Bartlemas remained wheezing on the floor as the bird circled to take another pass.

"Get up!" Jonathan shouted. He pointed through the museum's walkway to the main road beyond, where cars were criss-crossing by, unaware of the drama taking place only a few hundred metres away. "If we can reach the road, we'll be safe!"

Forcing the watchmaker to his feet, Jonathan dragged him across the colonnaded path, the low ceiling forcing the Phoenix to pull up and fly over the top of the museum. Bursting out the other side of the walkway, Jonathan led Bartlemas down a straight gravel path towards the main road. Although they were close enough to hear the rumbling buses, Jonathan felt the icy shadow of the Phoenix threatening to envelop him once more. From somewhere he found another spurt of energy, even though it felt like his chest was going to explode.

As they reached the main gates of the museum, a limousine with blacked-out windows pulled up in front of them. A rear door opened invitingly; Bartlemas dived inside without a second thought. Jonathan was about to follow suit, when he caught sight of the man in the back seat.

It was Vendetta.

Jonathan stopped in his tracks. This was the man he had been running from, the reason he had been dragged into this mystery. Now he was face to face with him, Jonathan wanted to turn on his heel and run in the opposite direction.

Bartlemas poked his head back out of the limousine, gesturing wildly for Jonathan to get in. Above his head, the Phoenix screeched with jubilation. As the cloud swooped down towards him, Jonathan heard the sounds of footsteps racing across the gravel towards the gate. Transfixed, he stood and stared at the cloud as it hurtled towards him. He wondered what death felt like – how much it would hurt.

He felt strong hands grabbing him.

"What are you waiting for?" Carnegie snarled. He manhandled Jonathan into the limousine and bundled in behind him.

With a squeal of tyres, the car raced away from the kerb, swerving through the lunch-time traffic. Through the rear window, Jonathan saw the black cloud pull up by the gates of the museum. There was an echoing screech of frustration, and then the darkness swept off towards the Thames.

Jonathan sat back in his seat, too exhausted to feel relief. As the adrenaline in his system drained away, his limbs felt like lead weights. Next to him, Carnegie was panting raggedly, his body shaking as the beast within him receded and he returned to human form. Bartlemas's eyes were alive with shock, his hands clutching at the small wooden box as though his life depended upon it. By contrast, Vendetta eyed his three passengers with open amusement.

"Rough day?"

The vampire was dressed casually in a crisp white shirt and chinos – despite the time of year, a pair of sunglasses were pushed up on to his forehead. He imbued the back of the car with the cold, lifeless smell of a morgue. Jonathan couldn't believe he was sitting only inches away from the creature who had tried to kill both him and his father. He was too tired to feel rage, though. If his life was going to end, he just hoped it would be quick.

"I've had rougher," Carnegie replied moodily. "Feel free to put that to the test."

"If you want a scuffle, go elsewhere," Vendetta shot back. "This is a limousine, not a bar room, Carnegie. You can at least feign civility, can't you?"

"That's rich!" Jonathan spluttered. "Coming from you!"

"You would do well to keep your mouth closed," the vampire said coldly. "I have hardly forgotten our past differences. Be grateful that for once, Starling, I feel less inclined to kill you than usual. Without your intervention, I'm not sure Bartlemas here would have made it."

"What *was* that thing?" asked the watchmaker. "I've never felt so scared."

"The Black Phoenix," Jonathan replied darkly. "It's a creature Lucien can transform into. It's utterly lethal."

"As James Ripper would testify," Vendetta added. "It seems that Darkside's first family have managed to get wind of our plan – we need to move quickly. Did you get the Chronos Wheel?"

Bartlemas nodded wearily, placing the wooden box in the vampire's hands. Vendetta opened the lid and pulled out a small, intricate piece of brass engineering. It looked exactly as it had on the watchmaker's diagram: three cogs with jagged teeth encircling a small sphere, the entire mechanism housed within a brass cage.

"I don't know what I was expecting," Vendetta said thoughtfully. "Something a little more . . . grandiose, perhaps."

"Don't be fooled," Bartlemas wheezed. "It may look like nothing, but it's utterly unique. It took my grandfather ten years to make it, you know, tapping into the darkest powers in Darkside." There was a note of pride in his voice as he went on. "Wilbur took its secret to the grave with him. He knew that no Lightsider could be trusted with its power. When he died, the Chronos Wheel was left to gather dust in the observatory. The only clue to its purpose lay in his coded notes, which remained in Darkside with my family. Only days ago was I able to break the code, and unlock the Chronos Wheel's secret."

"With a truly fitting sense of timing," Vendetta said. He closed the box with a snap, making the watchmaker jump. The vampire pressed a button on the intercom, and spoke crisply to the driver.

"Take us to the flat, Yann."

"Very good, sir," a dutiful voice buzzed back. Vendetta tapped his cheek thoughtfully with an elegant finger, and then turned to Bartlemas.

"And you're sure you can succeed where everyone has failed? You can make the Chronos Wheel work?"

"Given two, maybe three hours," the watchmaker replied confidently.

"Good. You can start as soon as we get back."

"I don't understand," Jonathan cut in. "What is the Chronos Wheel? What are you going to do with it?"

"I should have thought that would have been obvious," the vampire replied matter-of-factly. "We're going to bring James Ripper back from the dead."

18

"I hate to say it," Harry said, chewing thoughtfully on the end of his pencil, "but I'll be blowed if I know what we're going to do next."

Harry was perched on a stool in the back room of the Rook I'th Vine, poring over his notes. It was only early afternoon, but already the public house rang with raucous cries and bitter laughter. Although the Rook had a reputation as one of Darkside's milder drinking establishments, Raquella felt distinctly uncomfortable: as they waited at the bar for their drinks, men stared at her with open insolence; the bartender had sworn at Harry when he had asked for his change; and they had been pushed and jostled on their way to the table, froths of ale splashing over Raquella's shawl. Even now that they were safely seated, over Harry's shoulder the maid could see two footpads arguing violently over the divvying of their loot. Perhaps worst of all, the aroma of cinnamon wafting up from her cup of spiced water couldn't overcome the stench of sweat, smoke and spilled ale that steeped the walls and floorboards.

For once, however, Raquella kept her reservations to herself. It had been Harry's idea to come here, and she felt that she owed him something. After all, not only had he saved her from the hobgoblin, but he'd been thoughtful enough to remove the body while Raquella had got dressed. Harry didn't say exactly where he'd disposed of it, and the maid didn't press the matter. Instead she had gracefully agreed with his suggestion that they escape the gloomy confines of the Heights and walk down into the heart of Darkside. And then, instead of complaining about the shabbiness of the Rook, she had filled him in on the conversation with Vendetta.

Now Raquella blew on her cup, and took a careful sip of spiced water.

"I'm not sure if there's anything we *can* do next," she admitted, struggling to make herself heard over the din. "Vendetta is in Lightside. Bartlemas is in Lightside. Jonathan and Carnegie are in Lightside. We're in the wrong place."

"Perhaps," Harry said, underlining something in his notes. "There is one thing we could follow up here, though. Vendetta said he thought Holborn was paying Pelham to spy on him. What I want to know is – why?"

"My master and Holborn have never seen eye to eye. I wouldn't be surprised if the Abettor wanted to plant a spy in his household."

"In the middle of the Blood Succession?" Harry replied doubtfully. "If Holborn has sided with Lucien, I'd have thought he'd have other things on his mind right now. It doesn't quite add up for me. You worked with Pelham – what was he like?"

Raquella shrugged. "I never really got to find out. He kept himself to himself. He didn't seem like a bad person – but then, this is Darkside."

"Did he mention any friends, family? Someone we could talk to?"

"Not to me. . ." Raquella paused, the hubbub around her fading into the background as a faint memory pushed its way to the front of her mind. "Hold on – when we talked to Dexter Scabble down at Devil's Wharf, he said that he knew Mr Pelham from the No'penny Poorhouse. He mentioned a niece, Clara. I suppose there's a chance she might know something."

Harry raised his glass. "See? Maybe we're in the right place after all. Cheers!"

From the outside, the No'penny Poorhouse looked like just another factory, a functional, oblong building several storeys high, its walls lined with barred windows. In the early evening, as the clock approached seven, the street would be filled with bedraggled applicants hoping to gain entrance before the poorhouse shut it doors, but for now the road was deserted. Though the poorhouse was located in one of the bleakest parts of the borough, Raquella was simply glad to be outside. After the rank odour of the Rook, the stale breeze whipping across the cobblestones smelled like a fragrant flower.

They came to a halt by the main doors, uncertain of their next move.

"How are we going to get in here?" Raquella asked. "They don't just let anyone waltz inside, you know."

Harry scratched his head, sizing up the building. "The usual combination of stealth and subtlety, I'd imagine."

With that, he turned and began hammering his fists on the front door.

"LET US IN!" he bellowed. "At this rate Granddad'll be dead before we get to see him!"

There was a startled commotion inside, and then the door opened a crack. A cadaverous porter poked his head outside, blinking suspiciously in the light.

"What on Darkside is all this fuss about?" He stopped, surprised at the sight of the two teenagers. "What do you two want?"

"It's Granddad's birthday, and we want to sing happy birthday to him. Let us in, will you?"

"This ain't the Cain Club, you know," the porter snapped. "No visitors!"

Before he could withdraw his head and close the door, Harry's hands flashed out and grabbed hold of both of his ears, pulling him closer. The porter's face went bright red, and his eyes bulged.

"I don't think you understand," Harry said, his voice low

with menace. "We're here to see my granddad and I don't want to let my sister down. So let us in or you'll spend the rest of the day searching for your ears in the gutter. Understand?"

Nodding frantically, the porter yanked the door open. As Harry shoved him to one side and strode into the poorhouse, Raquella was suddenly reminded that – for all his casual jokes and easy arrogance – this was a Ripper standing alongside her. She followed him through the doorway, nagged by a sense of foreboding.

Raquella Joubert had grown up in the deprived back alleys of the Lower Fleet, part of a family that had been forced to scrap for every farthing. Yet the main hall of the No'penny Poorhouse presented her with a scene of abject poverty and utter need that she had never before encountered. She looked upon a seething menagerie of destitutes, their bony limbs barely covered by ragged clothing. Children scrabbled in the dirt, fighting over the vegetable remains splattered on the floor.

As Raquella skirted through the crowd, a buzz of excitement struck up: faces pitted with the ravages of smallpox looked up hopefully, praying for a charitable coin; toothless old women gabbled unintelligibly at her, pawing at her clothes; others kept their heads bowed, muttering their woes to themselves. Once Raquella cried out in shock when she stepped on a pile of rags on the floor, only for it to move and reveal a pale face. At her side, even Harry looked shaken by the scene.

They hurried through the main hall, unwilling to stop and speak to any of its inhabitants, only to find themselves in another room displaying precisely the same sights; and then another, and another. The noise and the smell and the squalor were unremitting. As they emerged from another packed room into a hallway marked by a staircase and a set of double doors, Raquella stopped and sank wearily to the ground.

"This is hopeless!" she groaned. "How are we ever going to find Mr Pelham's niece? There must be hundreds of people in here!"

"Don't give up just yet," urged Harry. "We just need a plan of attack, that's all." He pointed towards the double doors. "Look, you go that way, and see if you can get some sense out of anyone. I'll try upstairs. I'll meet you back here in ten minutes. If neither of us have any luck, we'll go back to the main hall together."

Before Raquella could argue with him, Harry was gone, slipping up the stairs like a shadow. Steeling herself for whatever lay ahead, Raquella pushed open the double doors and went inside the room beyond.

Although it was several seconds before her eyes adjusted to the gloom and she could make out the rows of beds lining the walls, Raquella knew instantly that she was in the infirmary. It was the atmosphere that gave it away: a thick fog of germs, hacking coughs and open sores, messy sneezes and festering wounds. Instinctively, she pressed her shawl over her mouth, fearful of what she might breathe in.

The infirmary was still and silent, its patients united in unspoken hopelessness. No one even stirred as Raquella passed by their beds.

On the verge of giving up hope altogether, Raquella called out: "Clara?"

She was rewarded with a movement in a bed on the other side of the room.

"Hello?" a voice replied tentatively.

Moving closer, Raquella saw that a girl had raised her head from the pillow and was peering out into the gloom. Although Clara was several years younger than the maid, a short lifetime of hardship had left her with a frail, skinny frame and a face lined with cares. She shrank back as Raquella approached.

"Who are you?" the girl asked fearfully. "How do you know my name?"

"Ssh!" Raquella said, placing a finger over her lips. "I'm a friend. You can trust me."

She sat down gingerly on the edge of the bed and took hold of the girl's hand.

"Do you know my Uncle Archie?" Clara said hopefully. "I haven't seen him for days. Not since the bad man came here."

Raquella leaned forward. "The bad man?"

Clara's face darkened. "He came here with Uncle Archie and threatened him. They thought I was asleep but I was listening. The bad man said if Uncle Archie didn't help him, I'd be sent away to a place worse than here." Clara's eyes moistened. "If there is a place worse than this, miss, I don't want to see it."

Raquella took off her shawl and placed it around the girl's shaking shoulders. "Of course you don't," she said soothingly. "And don't you worry – no one's going to send you anywhere."

From outside came the sound of marching footsteps, and a booming, self-important voice. Clara's head shot up.

"It's the warden! He's coming with the bad man, I know it!" she whispered. "You have to go!

Panic churning in her stomach, Raquella looked around for a hiding place. There were no cupboards to conceal her, no curtains to hide behind, no way past the iron bars that criss-crossed the windows. As the door handle turned and a crack of light entered the infirmary, Raquella leapt into the empty bed beside Clara's and pulled the musty sheet over her head. There she lay, stock-still, barely daring to breathe.

"Here we are, then," she heard the warden say briskly, even as Clara whimpered with fearful recognition. "I cannot thank you enough for once again gracing our humble institution with your presence."

"It is not a problem," a voice replied smoothly. "My ears are always listening out for the plaintive cries of the needy."

Beneath the sheets, Raquella's eyes widened. She would recognize that voice anywhere. The floorboards winced loudly as a pair of footsteps made a shuffling progress towards Clara's bed.

"Sit up, *ma cherie*, and take a deep breath," the voice continued. "There's a good child. . ."

It was Vendetta's doctor: Hugo La Mort.

19

Raquella held her breath beneath the sheet, questions racing through her mind. La Mort was the bad man Clara had been talking about? But why would the doctor need a spy in Vendetta's household? Weren't the two of them supposed to be friends?

On the other side of the ward, the warden was lecturing to his inmates, oblivious to the fact that no one was listening to him. From the bed next to her, Raquella heard La Mort whispering into Clara's ear.

"Bad news, child," the doctor hissed. "Your uncle let me down. It was not a difficult thing that I asked of him. Now I have had to make alternative arrangements, which have greatly inconvenienced me. I warned him, *ma cherie*, what would happen to you if he failed me. I have to keep my side of the bargain, *non*?"

"Where's Uncle Archie? What have you done to him?" Clara whimpered, before bursting into racking sobs.

Disturbed by the noise, the warden broke off from his sermon and approached the girl's bed.

"There, there. It's only the doctor. Hmm . . . what do you think, Doctor La Mort?"

"Oh, *monsieur* warden," La Mort replied, his voice honeyed with false concern, "this is a very sad case. I fear the girl's malady has spread to the brain. She is distressed, mentally enfeebled. I do not think there is much more a medical man can do for her, if you understand me?"

There was a pause.

"I see," the warden said slowly. "You think she would be more comfortable in the Bedlam?"

Clara made a small, horrified sound; Raquella's blood froze. Ever since she had been a little girl, the maid had heard the tales – the horror stories – of the Bedlam, Darkside's asylum for the insane. Everyone in the borough knew of its dreadful reputation, how decades of echoing screams and cries for help had warped the very walls themselves. Confining madmen to the Bedlam was a dark enough duty; committing someone who was sane was simply monstrous.

"Alas, I do," La Mort replied. "After my rounds I will come up to your office and sign the necessary papers, *oui*? But let us see if there are any patients here I can actually help." He turned towards the next bed. "What is the problem with this child?"

"To tell you the truth," the warden said, "I'm not entirely sure. It must be a new arrival."

"Well then, let us see what we are dealing with."

Footsteps drew near Raquella's bed. Her heart pounded; she knew she was trapped. If La Mort saw her face, there was no telling what he might do to her. Raquella felt the doctor take hold of the bed sheet and try to pull it down. She resisted, her knuckles blanching with the effort. All the while a single thought was revolving around her brain: where on Darkside was Harry?

"It seems," La Mort grunted, "that this one is suffering from an acute case of shyness."

"Not shyness," Clara said, in a small voice. "Typhus. That's why she's trying to stay away from you."

The doctor suddenly released his grip on the sheet.

"What did you say?" La Mort said.

"She was brought in about an hour ago. I heard them say she had typhus. She won't be long with us now. . ."

"Doctor La Mort," the warden cut in hastily, "I assure you, there is no way that—"

"*Sacre bleu!*" the doctor exclaimed violently. "You imbecile! You incompetent! I offer you my services, my expertise, and you reward me by enclosing me in this . . . this *death trap*! This patient should be in an isolation room on her own! Do you have any idea how infectious typhus is? I could already have caught it!"

"Please, *monsieur* doctor, you have to believe me—"

There was the sound of a ringing slap, and the warden cried out. A pair of footsteps stormed out of the room, hurriedly followed by another, and then the infirmary door slammed shut. Breathing a deep sigh of relief, Raquella pulled the sheet back from her head. She smiled at Clara.

"That was brilliant," she said. "Thank you."

Clara tried to smile, but the tears were still rolling down her face.

"Oh, Clara," Raquella said tenderly, "I'm so sorry about your uncle."

"He's gone, miss," Clara sniffed. "He's gone, and I'm alone, and they're going to send me to the madhouse. And I ain't mad, miss! Honest!"

Raquella got out of the bed and hastened to the girl's side.

"I know you're not mad, Clara. And you're not on your own. I'm here, and I'll make sure that no one sends you to the madhouse. Can you walk?"

"I can try, miss, but where are we going to go?"

"Outside—"

The doors to the infirmary crashed open. Light poured into the room, outlining the familiar silhouette of Harry Pierce.

". . . And this nice gentleman is going to help us."

Harry paced impatiently into the room, peering into the beds.

"Is that you, Raquella?" he called out. "I said ten minutes! What have you been doing?"

"I could ask you the same question," Raquella shot back. "Come on, Clara."

She helped the girl climb out of bed, wrapping the

shawl tightly around Clara as she tottered to her feet. Harry looked on, frowning.

"Is that Clara?"

"It is," Raquella replied firmly, helping the little girl as she hobbled towards Harry. "She's coming with us."

"Is that really a good idea? We've got to get out of here, you know, and this really isn't the best time. . ."

He broke off. Even the dingy light couldn't obscure the look on Raquella's face.

"Harry Pierce," she said, in a voice several degrees below freezing, "either this girl comes with us or you can walk out on your own. It's entirely up to you. But leave us now, and I will take out a full-page advert in the *Informer* telling the entire borough what a coward you are. Are we clear on that point?"

A look passed over Harry's face that Raquella didn't recognize. With a jolt, she realized it was embarrassment.

"Right. Sorry about that. Perhaps I can help here?"

He picked up Clara's tiny form as though she were made of straw, and hoisted her into his arms. At the infirmary doors, Harry paused and nodded for Raquella to go before him. She swished past him, head held high.

"Better, Harry. Much better."

If anything, the poorhouse was getting busier – the corridor outside was crammed with paupers shouting and bickering with one another. They had barely taken ten paces when there came a shout from behind them.

"Hey! You there!"

Raquella looked over her shoulder to see the cadaverous porter from the front gate hastening after them with a pompous red-faced man, who she presumed was the warden, at his side. They were ominously flanked by two large guards carrying billy clubs. The red-faced man called out again.

"Yes, you! I want to speak with you!"

"Harry," Raquella said softly to her companion, "I think we may need to go a little faster."

"How much faster?"

Raquella turned again, to see the warden pointing them out to the two guards, who began lumbering in their direction.

"I think running would be a start," she said.

"I had a nasty feeling you were going to say that," Harry sighed, shifting Clara in his arms. "Follow me."

With that, he darted off down a side corridor, dodging through the gaggles of people and hurdling prone bodies. Even with the burden of Clara in his arms, Harry was fast – Raquella could only just keep pace with him. The guards barrelled their way along the corridor after them, shouldering people out of the way, clubbing anyone unfortunate enough to block their path.

"They're gaining on us!" she cried desperately.

"Can't go any faster!" Harry shouted back. "We've got to slow them down!"

They burst into the main hall, which was now so full of bodies it resembled a solid mass of human flesh. Harry cursed and tried to push his way through the throng, but with his arms full it was difficult to make an impression. Raquella knew that, although they were within touching distance of the main entrance, they would never make it. In the centre of the hall she came to a halt, and turned to face their pursuers.

"Are you mad?" Harry shouted. "They'll kill you! Come on!"

Raquella pulled out a small pouch from the folds of her dress and undid the drawstring, her fingers shaking. She pulled out a handful of coins and hurled them high into the air towards the guards, their edges glinting in the fading afternoon light. The shocked hall fell into a silence so profound that the only sound was the tinkling of the coins as they hit the floor at the guards' feet.

Then all hell broke loose.

With a roar of desire, the paupers descended on the coins like a swarm of bees. Besieged, the guards began swinging their clubs about their heads, but there were too many opponents to quell. As the punches and the kicks and bites rained down upon them, the guards were quickly swallowed up in the scrum, until their swinging clubs could no longer be seen, and their cries for help could be heard no more.

Raquella looked on, frozen by the chaos she had created. She felt a hand on her shoulder. It was Harry. The boy had put Clara down, and was looking sympathetically into Raquella's eyes.

"It was the only way," the maid said softly. "I had to do something. . ."

"I know," he replied. "It's time to go."

Taking her hand, Harry gently led the two girls towards the exit, leaving the No'penny Poorhouse to its bleak fate.

It was dark by the time they reached the offices of the *Darkside Informer*. Harry climbed wearily up the stairs and deposited Clara into the care of Arthur Blake. The pudgy editor took one look at the young girl and immediately took charge, ordering one of his employees to race out into the streets and bring back hot food and drink. Now she was upstairs in his office, wrapped in one of Arthur's oversized coats, giggling as the editor made shadow animals dance across the walls.

Down in the main office, Raquella found herself wishing that someone would take similar care of her. The poorhouse had overwhelmed her in a way that the horrors of Vendetta's service never had. She couldn't shake the images of the starving families and feral children from her head. Now, sitting with Harry at his desk, Vendetta's ledger between them, she suddenly felt very, very tired.

She looked up to see Harry eyeing her with concern.

"Are you all right?" he asked.

"I'm fine," Raquella said, a hint of irritation creeping into her voice. "Don't worry about me. I'm just trying to make sense of what happened. I can't work out why the doctor would cross Vendetta."

"There, I might be able to help you," Harry said. "What was his name again?"

"The doctor? Hugo La Mort. Why, do you know him?"

"No," he replied, opening the ledger and leafing through the pages, "but I've seen his name before. A few hundred times, in fact. I've read this book from cover to cover, and Hugo La Mort turns up again and again. He makes large regular payments to one person – the same man every time. Can you guess who?"

Suddenly, things started to become clearer in Raquella's mind. "Vendetta."

"The one and only. Here – check out these entries." Harry turned the ledger round, showing her the payments. It was clear that, over the years, Vendetta had received a large sum of money from the doctor.

"So La Mort was paying my master. But what does it mean?"

Harry shrugged. "Damned if I know. But I think it might be worth paying a visit to the good doctor's house."

"Is that wise?" Raquella said doubtfully, casting a glance at the grandfather clock by the wall. "La Mort works through the night, you know. He could still be up."

Harry smiled grimly.

"Even better," he said.

20

As Vendetta's limousine purred along a dockside road south of the Thames, the silence in the back of the car was broken by Carnegie's harsh laughter.

"You're insane," said the wereman.

The vampire arched an eyebrow. "Do you really think so? I have been accused of many things in the past, but madness has never been one of them."

"James has been dead for twelve years!" Carnegie guffawed. "He'll be a rotting corpse, for Ripper's sake!"

"I wouldn't expect you to grasp the intricacies of this plan, wolfman," Vendetta said icily. "After all, its architect was Thomas Ripper himself."

"So what do you have to do with it, then?" the wereman asked.

"Several weeks after James's death, I was summoned to Blackchapel in the middle of the night. Thomas met me in a secret chamber behind the throne room. Even then, I could see the beginnings of his decline. He was still a broad, imposing figure – he had killed all three of his brothers in armed combat, lest you forget – but his spirit had been broken. Alas, even the Rippers are human."

"Barely," Jonathan muttered, his thoughts turning back to the Black Phoenix.

"That night," the vampire continued, "Thomas confided in me that he felt James had been his true heir, and that he feared neither of his remaining children were fit to take the throne. He told me of his plan to try and resurrect James. Thomas needed help arranging the operation, and it was common knowledge that James and I were friends. I was a natural ally.

"The next few months were . . . not easy. Thomas was a man possessed; there were no lengths to which he wouldn't go to raise his own son. He took me down to the deepest cellars in Darkside, where cursed crones committed sacrifices in the hope of gaining power. We saw things beyond your wildest imagination and your worst dreams, Starling, but all to no avail. The soul of James Ripper remained beyond our reach."

"And then you met me," Josiah said proudly.

Vendetta glared at the watchmaker, piqued by the interruption. "Bartlemas managed to convince me that he could build a mechanism capable of turning back not just time, but life itself. I arranged the payments from Thomas, and oversaw his efforts. Initially progress was slow, the prototypes worse than useless. All the while Thomas was slowly dying, a deeply frustrated man."

"And then I managed to crack the code in my grandfather's diaries," Bartlemas babbled excitedly. "I discovered that the Chronos Wheel could provide the solution to our problems – if we could only get it to work. Two essential components were missing. For one thing, the Wheel needed to be encased in moonstone . . ."

". . . which Dexter Scabble was good enough to provide you with," Carnegie said.

Vendetta inclined his head. "Indeed. And I found the second component on Lightside. Now Bartlemas has all he needs to bring the Wheel to life."

"It is just a shame that Thomas didn't live long enough to see his dream realized," the watchmaker added.

"If he had survived for one more week. . ." Vendetta said. He smiled coldly. "Perhaps there is something to be said for being dead already."

"Still sounds like a fool's errand to me," Carnegie growled.

A flicker of irritation showed on the vampire's face, and then he settled back in his seat.

"Of course, you would know best," he mocked. "But why don't you indulge me? Come with us and see for yourself. We've nearly arrived at my flat."

Jonathan looked out through the tinted windows to see a vast building swallowing up his view. The limousine moved through the front entrance and made its way towards a forbidding set of metal gates at the back of the building. The gates parted as the car approached, and it rolled down a slope into an underground garage, a gloomy mausoleum of expensive sports cars. As they eased into a reserved parking space near the exit, Vendetta got out and strode towards the lift, Bartlemas scuttling along in his wake. Jonathan caught Carnegie's arm as the wereman made to follow.

"What are you doing?" he hissed. "This is the guy who's been chasing after me, remember? Now you want to go up to his flat?"

Carnegie nodded at the receding figure of Vendetta. "Doesn't look like he's too bothered with you now, boy. You can get out of here any time you want. Me, I'm going to see what he's up to."

The wereman walked away, the sound of throat-clearing echoing around the garage. Jonathan stood on his own for a few seconds, tapping his foot with consternation, before racing after him. He caught the lift doors just as they were closing and squeezed inside, ensuring that Carnegie was between him and Vendetta. The four of them were sandwiched together uncomfortably as the lift rose to the top floor, before disgorging them inside the penthouse suite.

Jonathan found himself standing in a spacious split-level flat with polished wooden floorboards. Heavy shutters guarded the windows, preventing even the faintest beam of sunlight from slipping inside. Here and there were light bulbs on thin black stands – without lampshades to soften their glow, they burned with a piercing white light. Save for a few chairs, a low table and a giant television screen, there were barely any furnishings. No paintings or mirrors hung on the whitewashed walls. As in the limousine, there was an antiseptic atmosphere that Jonathan found more unpleasant than the smell of grime and raw meat that clogged the air in Carnegie's lodgings. It reminded him of the hospital where he used to visit his dad. But, for all his misgivings, he knew that the flat must have been worth millions.

Carnegie looked around the austere surroundings and scratched his cheek thoughtfully.

"Very . . . clean," he sniffed.

Vendetta inclined his head, as though receiving a compliment. "I still have business to conduct in Lightside, and I am accustomed to a certain level of comfort. Of course, it is not the Heights, but it suffices."

Prising open the shutters, Jonathan saw a balcony looking out over the grim, grey swirls of the Thames.

"Nice view," he said.

"By night," the vampire replied curtly, snapping the shutters closed. He turned round, fixing Bartlemas with a steely glare. "You have the Wheel. The moonstone is in the room next door. Why are you still here?"

The watchmaker nodded, and hurried off into the adjoining room.

Carnegie wiped his nose on his sleeve. "So what do we do now?"

"We wait," Vendetta said.

The vampire picked up a remote control and turned on his television, the giant plasma screen displaying a bright, bustling newsroom. A smartly dressed woman was addressing the camera.

"And now we return to our main story – the disturbances at the Greenwich Observatory earlier this afternoon. Eyewitnesses have reported gunshots and a sudden eclipse. Joining us now is Detective Horace Carmichael from the Metropolitan Police Force. Detective Carmichael, can you shed any light on today's bizarre events?"

Jonathan blinked. There in the television studio, looking uneasy in the glare of the spotlights, was the familiar face of the hunchbacked detective.

"Obviously it's early days," Carmichael began, "and we're still collecting statements, but our initial enquiries are strongly suggesting that this was some sort of prank – possibly a group of environmental activists trying to gain some publicity for their cause."

"So you're not taking the reports of gunfire seriously, then?" the newsreader pressed.

"We take any disturbance of this nature seriously," Carmichael replied, "and the Metropolitan Police will be investigating this further, but it's important to stress to the public that we think this is the work of a few misguided individuals, rather than anything more sinister."

"Thank you, Detective. Now, in other news. . ."

Carnegie snorted. "Lightsiders. If they stuck their heads in the sand any deeper, they'd get it between their toes."

"Don't be so sure," Jonathan said slowly. "I've met

Carmichael before, remember? He wasn't like other policemen. Don't you remember what happened after we carried out the robbery in Kensington? Carmichael said they'd caught the people who did it, but they never mentioned us once. It's like he was covering it up."

"For once, Starling's right," Vendetta said. "It's not in everyone's interests for Darkside to become public knowledge, Carnegie. Although it may take a little more subtlety than you have at your disposal to understand why."

"Subtlety is overrated," Carnegie shot back.

For a few seconds a challenge hung in the air, until Vendetta chuckled hollowly and went to pour himself a glass of mineral water. Carnegie stomped out on to the balcony, where he spent the next few hours moodily watching the Thames trudge by. Jonathan tried to lose himself watching television, but he couldn't relax with the vampire in the room. Despite Carnegie's apparent lack of concern, Jonathan couldn't shake the suspicion that at any second Vendetta might attack him.

It was a relief when Bartlemas finally came scurrying back into the room, sleeves rolled up and hands covered in grease.

"It is ready!" he exclaimed.

"And not before time," Vendetta snapped. "You are sure it will work?"

"As sure as I can be," Bartlemas replied. "But I cannot be certain until we go to James's grave."

"I've never tried to bring the dead back to life before,"

Carnegie began pointedly, "but wouldn't it be a good idea to test that Wheel first?"

"We cannot test it," Bartlemas protested. "We have only so much. . ." The watchmaker broke off.

A shiver of premonition ran down Jonathan's spine.

"Only so much what?" he asked, in a small voice. "You said there were two things needed to make the Wheel work. What was the second? Why *were* you on Lightside, Vendetta?"

Bartlemas's eyes glinted. "You have to understand, Jonathan – this watch needs a power that goes beyond coils and cogs. A deeper, more elemental power than engineering alone can provide. That was the secret of my grandfather's invention, why no one else could get it to work."

Carnegie's eyes narrowed. "What are you saying?"

"The watch reverses life," Vendetta said matter-of-factly. "To do so, it needs a life of its own. It needs to be oiled with blood." He turned and smiled at Jonathan. "And, given the very special circumstances, very special blood. Specifically, that of a half-Darksider."

Jonathan's heart sank.

"You wanted the boy," Carnegie said hoarsely. "That's why you were so pleased to see us."

Vendetta nodded slowly. "I'll admit, I did pay a visit to the boy's school when I first crossed over. Half-breeds are a rarity, and I didn't have the time to cast my net around. As luck would have it, however, I found another solution. Come with me."

The vampire turned on his heel and led them down a long corridor to a heavy iron door barricaded with three planks of wood.

"As I mentioned earlier, I do conduct a lot of business in Lightside. I have found it expedient to make some special . . . alterations to the flat." Vendetta smiled. "You never know when you might have guests."

He lifted off the planks and pushed open the door. Jonathan crept forward, his heart pounding, into a circular room. Two flaming torches faced each other, their flickering tongues of light brushing across a dark chasm that lay in the centre of the floor between them. Taken aback by the medieval scene, Jonathan had to remind himself that he was still in modern London.

He inched forward to the edge of the pit and peered cautiously over the edge, nervous that some kind of foul creature was chained up there. Instead, he was stunned to see a bedraggled girl in her school uniform slumped at the bottom. She looked up at the sound of his footsteps, and suddenly everything became horribly clear.

"Tell me, Starling," Vendetta said pleasantly. "Have you met Kate?"

21

For two days, Kate Riley had fled from one nightmare to the next, pursued through her unconscious by Vendetta. She saw the vampire's incisors glinting in the darkness, heard his mocking laughter at her repeated prayers that this couldn't be happening to her. Everywhere she turned, in the murky, shifting landscapes of her dreams, he was there.

Finally, Kate woke up. There was a sour taste in her mouth, and she had a pounding headache. Lifting her head from the stone floor, she saw that she was lying at the bottom of a pit. High above her head she could see two burning torches, but their light failed to penetrate the depths of the pit. Kate shivered. The room was deathly cold.

"Hello?" she called out timidly, unsure whether or not she wanted a reply. "Is anyone there?"

Silence.

As the reality of her situation hit home, Kate could feel

her chest tighten with dread. In an effort to stay calm, she took a series of long, deep breaths. Panicking wasn't going to get her anywhere. At least she was alive. When Vendetta had closed in on her in the technology workshop, she had thought she was done for. The important thing now was getting out of the pit. It was nearly twice as deep as she was tall, and the walls were hopelessly smooth – there were no helpful handholds enabling her to climb out. Vendetta appeared to have taken away her school bag, and her mobile phone with it. Kate was totally trapped.

She wondered where she was – whether she was even still in London. Her parents would be frantic with worry: had they gone to the police, or organized search parties? Thinking of her parents made Kate feel vulnerable again, and she hurriedly turned her mind to something else. Wherever she was, surely someone had to be in earshot.

"HELP!" she screamed at the top of her lungs, until she felt dizzy. "HELP!"

After a couple of minutes, a door creaked open and she heard soft footsteps approach the pit. Kate's stomach lurched with fear.

"Who's . . . who's there?" she said.

An object came flying down towards her from out of the gloom. Kate screamed and shielded her face with her hands, only to see a water bottle bounce harmlessly at her feet. She heard a man chuckle.

"I thought you might need some refreshment," Vendetta's voice floated down. "Screaming is such thirsty work. By all means continue. This flat is soundproofed – the only person who'll hear is me, and I find the sound rather soothing."

"Why am I here?" Kate asked warily. "What do you want with me?"

"All in good time, girl. You'll see soon enough."

The footsteps retreated from the room, and Kate was alone once more. She resumed her search for a way out with renewed vigour, but it was hopeless. She banged the walls with her fists in frustration, and slumped back to the floor. She felt weary, and her head still hurt, but there wasn't enough room in the pit to stretch out comfortably. Instead she sat back and waited, rationing her sips of water. There wasn't any food to eat, but that didn't matter – Kate was too tense to feel hungry.

Down in the pit, time began to lose all meaning. Eventually the door creaked open again, and she heard someone enter the room. This time, when she looked up into the flickering torchlight, she saw the shocked face of Jonathan Starling staring back at her.

"Kate?" he asked incredulously. "Are you all right?"

Not trusting herself to answer without bursting into tears, she nodded numbly. Jonathan looked back towards the doorway, his voice hard.

"What she's doing down there?"

"I've already told you," Vendetta replied, an undertow of amusement in his voice. "I went to your school to find you, only to have the unexpected pleasure of making Kate's acquaintance. Given that she's a half-Darksider too, I thought I'd use her instead. Really, Starling, I should have thought this would be good news for you."

"She's a *what*?"

Suddenly Vendetta appeared at the rim of the pit. He gestured down towards Kate.

"A half-Darksider – can't you sense it? Can't you hear the blood pounding in her veins, struggling to get free? The crashing waves of your own turbulent heritage? The sound echoes in my ears, Starling."

As Kate struggled to comprehend what was going on, Jonathan squared up to the vampire. If the boy was intimidated, he hid it well.

"I don't care what you think she is – get her out of there, now."

The room echoed to the sound of Vendetta's mocking laughter. "I'm not sure you're in a position to be giving me orders, Starling. I will do exactly what I want with the girl, whether you like it or not."

"The watch," Jonathan said suddenly, in a quiet voice. "You're going to use her. . ." His voice trailed off, and he looked away from Kate.

"What?" she called out, her voice cracking. "You're going to use my *what*?"

"Let her go," Jonathan said firmly. "Take me instead."

Vendetta raised an eyebrow. "What an interesting suggestion! I can't pretend using you wouldn't give me more satisfaction, although I did promise Kate. . . Come to think of it, seeing as you're both currently guests of mine, I might as well take the pair of you. I can make up my mind on the way."

Kate jumped as a loud snarl rang out above her head, and a large man with something animal about him pushed his way in front of Jonathan and pointed at the vampire. He spoke in a low, gravelly voice that grated with menace.

"If you think I'm going to let either of them come to harm, you'd better think again."

"More threats," Vendetta sighed. "It seems you and the boy can't let a minute pass without some kind of blustering warning. Let me assure you of one thing – we are travelling to James's grave this evening, and one of them is going to power the watch. Perhaps we should discuss this next door?"

The unkempt man stomped angrily out of the room, followed by Vendetta. Kate looked up in desperation at Jonathan as he lingered at the edge of the pit.

"We'll get you out of this, Kate – I promise."

"Don't leave me in here! Please!"

"I'll be back as soon as I can. You're safe for now."

With that, Jonathan disappeared from view.

"PLEASE!" Kate screamed, but the only reply was the faltering of the torches as the door slammed shut and the thud of the planks as they were lifted back into place across it. Kate fell to the floor, and this time she couldn't stop the tears from coming.

*

They returned for her later, by which time she had managed to compose herself. Jonathan's face reappeared at the edge of the pit, his large, bristling companion at his shoulder. The man dangled the end of a rope down towards her.

"Wrap it under your arms and I'll lift you up," he barked.

Kate did as she was told just in time, finishing the knot as the rope bit into her armpits and she was jerked into the air. The man hauled her hand-over-hand up to the lip of the pit, whereupon Jonathan reached out to guide her on to solid ground. Kate caught her breath as they untied the rope, feeling as though she could breathe properly for the first time in days. A hand touched her on the shoulder.

"My name's Carnegie," the man growled. "Can you walk?"

Kate nodded. She was so relieved to be out of the pit that she could have kissed his weathered face. "Where are we going?"

There came a polite cough from the doorway. Kate turned and saw Vendetta leaning against the door frame. The vampire was carrying a snub-nosed pistol, which was pointed straight at Jonathan's heart.

"He can tell you in the car," Vendetta said. "It's dark now. We haven't got time to waste."

They were marched out of the flat and down to an underground car park, where a spindly old man was waiting for them by a limousine. Vendetta ordered them into the back of the car with the new man, who, Kate couldn't help but notice, guiltily refused to meet her eye. There was a heavy click as the doors locked shut, and then the vampire's voice buzzed over the intercom.

"I thought I'd take the front seat this time," he said breezily. "Do make yourself at home."

Jonathan and Carnegie exchanged a dark look.

"I told you we should have made a break for it," the boy said, rattling the door lock futilely. "I don't understand why we're still here."

"We had to get the girl free before we could try to escape," Carnegie growled. "*I* don't understand why you're so confused."

"Well, I don't understand *anything*." Kate laughed incredulously. "Do you think you could tell me what's going on – please?"

And so, as the limousine drove over Tower Bridge and through the city centre of London, Jonathan told her – a dizzying, impossible tale of fantastical creatures and dark secrets rendered even more incredible by the fact that Kate could look out of the car window at the late-night shoppers hurrying past familiar London landmarks, blissfully unaware of the world that was being described.

When Jonathan had finished, Kate sat back in her seat, overwhelmed.

"Listen," he said. "I'm really sorry you got dragged into this."

"It's my fault, not yours," Kate said ruefully. "I was the one who started sticking my nose in."

"Believe me, if Vendetta's right about you being half-Darkside, you can't help it. I was just the same."

"I guess," Kate shrugged. "He seems pretty sure about me, anyway."

"How are you finding it so far?"

Kate pretended to think about it. "So far? To be honest – not that great."

But despite the dangerous situation, a part of Kate was relieved to learn about her background, as though an itch in the back of her mind had finally been scratched. Her restless turbulence, the strange kinship she had felt with Jonathan, even the problems at home – everything seemed to make a little more sense now.

The limousine had left the centre of London, and was now purring down a sharply inclining street that cut a passage between a set of iron railings and a row of grand houses. At the bottom of the hill, the car pulled into a cobbled lay-by near a side gate in the railings. The door locks clicked open, and suddenly Vendetta was gesturing with his pistol for them to get out.

"I recognize this place!" Jonathan exclaimed into the night air. "This is Highgate Cemetery!"

The vampire nodded. "Because James was slain before the Succession, tradition forbids his family from burying him in Darkside alongside his ancestors. Thomas arranged for him to be buried here in Highgate. I was there when they crossed over one night and committed him to the earth."

Vendetta unlocked the gates and led them inside the cemetery. A broad pathway curved gently around a bank of graves, which sloped up and into the trees. The silence was as absolute as the darkness. Kate tiptoed through the shadows of towering Celtic crosses, and past angels clasping their hands together in prayer, their stone faces weathered and stern. In certain places the graves were arranged haphazardly, almost on top of one another, bundling their inhabitants together in death.

The vampire walked quickly, as though retreading a familiar journey, before coming to a fork in the path marked by an obelisk-shaped grave. He pointed to a set of narrow steps which had been cut into the bank between two graves, leading away from the main pathway before disappearing amongst the trees.

"We go this way," Vendetta said crisply. "After you."

After a deep breath, Kate climbed up the bank, trying to avoid the feeling that she was trespassing over dead bodies. The crude steps led deeper into the undergrowth, where trees creaked and leaves rustled in the breeze. Even surrounded by death, it was hard not to feel as though there was life up here: a wild, dark force of nature. Her heart thumping in her chest, Kate heard Jonathan pressing along behind her, and took comfort from his presence.

A rough trail continued through a row of increasingly ornate graves that had fallen into disrepair: the stonework was chipped, the engravings swallowed up by moss. Finally

Kate came out into a small glade, marked by a mound of earth in the centre of the clearing.

"We are here," Vendetta announced. "The last resting place of James Ripper. Now we can begin. . ."

22

The rain had eased, leaving the pavements and cobblestones in Jackdaw Square glistening in the glow of the street lamps. Even in normal, rowdier times, this more refined district preferred to carry out its crimes in private, behind thick curtains and oak-panelled doors. Now, just after midnight in the midst of the Blood Succession, the houses were united in a conspiratorial silence.

Presently, the door to one of the houses opened, briefly spilling light out on to the square, and a small man waddled down into a waiting carriage. With a loud giddy-up, the coachman spurred the horses into life, and the carriage rattled off into the night. As the sound died away, two figures dressed in black emerged from the shadows by the park railings and sized up the house in front of them.

"Where do you think he's gone?" Raquella whispered.

Harry shrugged. "As long as it's somewhere far away, I don't care."

Pulling out his lock picks, the boy darted across the

street and set to work on Dr Hugo La Mort's front door. Raquella kept a nervous lookout, convinced that at any second the lights would flick on in a neighbouring house, or a cry of alarm would go up. With the Bow Street Runners still abroad, this was the worst time to be caught committing a crime in Darkside.

After what seemed like an age, Harry made a small sound of satisfaction, and the lock clicked open. He ushered Raquella inside the residence and quietly closed the door behind them.

"Try not to disturb anything," he urged in a low voice. "We don't want the doctor knowing we've been here, if we can help it."

"Yes, thank you, Harry," the maid replied stiffly. "You are aware this isn't my first burglary?"

The boy looked surprised for a second, and then grinned. "You're a girl after my own heart, Raquella."

She turned away, unwilling to give Harry the satisfaction of a reaction. Remembering the eerie encounter in the doctor's study the last time she had been here, Raquella was unwilling to head straight upstairs. Instead, she led Harry around the ground floor, where they began combing for clues. The kitchen and front room were dark and dormant, but a lamp was still burning in the back room, and as she entered, the maid saw a sheaf of papers on the desk. Raquella pulled up a chair and began carefully leafing through them.

Most of the papers were letters from patients: angry

accusations of malpractice and injury, the handwriting wobbly and the pages stained with blood; veiled threats of retribution; heartfelt pleas on behalf of sick loved ones. At the bottom of the pile, however, was a letter written on aged, yellowed paper, on which Raquella instantly recognized the smooth, controlled handwriting of her master. She called Harry over, and the pair of them began to read:

Vendetta Heights
8 May, DY 114

My dear Hugo,

As both your friend and banker, it has fallen to me to inform you that your account at my bank has run out of credit. It would appear that your fondness for games of chance at the Casino Sanguino has taken its toll. Have I not told you in the past, Hugo, that a wise man never gambles?

Usually in this situation, I would be taking certain punitive measures against you to retrieve your debt. Then again, I know you have no relatives I could harm, and your income depends upon you possessing both of your hands. Given our amicable relationship, I have decided to forestall the threat of violence, and instead arranged a very reasonable repayment plan. As a security, I have confiscated the key to your safety deposit box, which I know contains some items of great value to you. No doubt your desire to regain these items will spur you on to settle your debt sooner rather than later – just the sort of encouragement friends should provide for one another, don't you think?

Regards,

G. Vendetta

"I guess that explains La Mort's payments in the ledger," Harry said eventually. "He was paying back Vendetta."

Raquella nodded. "In a way, he was fortunate. My master is not always so understanding about debts."

"Still, when Vendetta visited La Mort and told him he was going away for a while, the good doctor saw an opportunity to get his deposit box back sooner than they'd agreed. So he goes to the poorhouse and forces Mr Pelham to start snooping around the Heights."

"Of course!" Raquella exclaimed. "The key! When we found the ledger in the secret room in the Heights, there was a key next to it. That's what Mr Pelham was looking for! He was so close!"

"Which means. . ."

"Which means I know where the key is! We can go and get it now, and open the box before La Mort gets his hands on it."

Harry put down the letter, frowning. "That's a point. If Vendetta caught Mr Pelham, and La Mort didn't get his hands on the key, what's the doctor been doing in the meantime?"

There came a low moan from upstairs. Harry and Raquella froze.

"There's someone here!" the maid mouthed, her eyes wide.

Harry nodded. "Sounds like they're in pain, too," he whispered.

Gesturing at Raquella to stay behind him, Harry pulled a long-handled dagger from his belt and crept back into the hallway, moving with the alert stealth of a cat. As he stole up the stairs, another pitiful moan wafted down from the doctor's study. Raquella stayed as close to Harry as she could, reassured by his cool composure. Although the maid didn't scare easily, there was something about the atmosphere in the still, stuffy house that chilled her to the core, and sent goosepimples scurrying across her skin.

The study door was ajar, allowing Harry to peer into the room before he entered. A gas lamp was still burning away, casting long shadows over the glass specimen jars and the gruesome diagrams on the wall. At first glance, the room appeared to be empty, but as Harry pushed the door further open, they heard the sound of whimpering coming from behind the floor-length curtain drawn across the back of the room.

Harry gestured at Raquella to wait by the doorway, and then moved soundlessly across the room. He grabbed hold of the curtain with one hand, raising his dagger with the other. The whimpering was louder now. Raquella had to fight the urge to cover her eyes.

Harry swept the curtain aside with a flourish, and took a sharp intake of breath.

In front of him sat a middle-aged man, tied into a chair with thick leather straps. On a tray next to the chair was the white porcelain bowl containing La Mort's surgical instruments. As she neared, Raquella was sickened to notice that they were gleaming with fresh blood. Harry quickly cut the leather straps with his dagger and helped the man up and into an armchair. He appeared to be in shock – his limbs were trembling, and he rocked back and forward in his chair, clasping his hands together. It wasn't until Raquella had poured him a large glass of brandy that he was able to speak.

"T-Thank you," he stammered.

"Who are you?" the maid asked gently. "What happened?"

"My name is Frederick Longbourne," the man answered bitterly. "Two days ago that . . . monster La Mort came into my shop, saying he wanted a spare key cut. When I turned to begin using my equipment, I felt a sharp stabbing pain in my neck, and everything went black. When I came to, I was strapped into this chair. La Mort was friendly at first. He told me he'd let me go after I'd given him what he wanted: a skeleton key to use in Vendetta's bank."

"A skeleton key?" Harry looked puzzled. "What's that?"

"It's a master key," replied Longbourne. "It has adjustable teeth, and can open any lock."

"Why didn't you just give it to him?" Raquella asked.

"It's not that simple. The skeleton key is the most prized possession of a locksmith, and his greatest secret. If it falls into the wrong hands, then anyone can open any door, and there are no uses for locks any more. When I refused to hand it over he became angry, and began to. . ."

Longbourne nodded at the instruments in the bowl, unable to say any more. Raquella shivered.

"I held out for as long as I could, but I could tell that time was running out for him. Tonight he lost patience and . . ." the locksmith shifted awkwardly in his chair, wincing with pain ". . . I couldn't take it any more. My skeleton key was hidden in a secret compartment in my belt buckle. He removed it and left immediately. Though not before he told me what he was going to do to me when he returned. La Mort is . . . inhuman."

Harry nodded. "It's amazing you resisted for as long as you did." He glanced at Raquella, and said crisply, "Take him to a real doctor. I'll go to the Heights and get the key, and then we can meet up back at the bank."

Loungbourne shook his head wearily. "There's no time for all that, don't you see? La Mort's gone to the bank now. Unless you go after him right away, he'll be long gone!"

"But we can't just leave you like this!" Raquella said.

"You've freed me – that's enough. It's more important that you stop him, whatever he's doing."

Harry nodded. As he and Raquella made to leave the study, the locksmith caught his arm. When Longbourne spoke this time, there was a cold, hard edge to his voice.

"If you find yourself up against La Mort, don't hesitate to hurt him."

"I don't think you have to worry about that," Harry replied ominously.

23

The Bank of Darkside was located at the bottom of Deadneedle Street, a broad thoroughfare that intersected with the northern end of the Grand. In the decades before the borough had been cold-shouldered by the rest of Victorian London, the building had been a church, and its spire still managed to raise a crooked salute to the sky. But instead of prayers and hymns, the bank now echoed with the jingle of coins and the ringing of tills.

Having flagged down a hansom cab outside Jackdaw Square, Raquella and Harry were now rattling along Deadneedle Street towards the bank. Even with the Blood Succession under way, night-time was still business time in the rotten borough, and the carriage overtook a mob of Darksiders heading for the same destination. Some clutched nervously at their money pouches, starting at the slightest noise, while others tried to deter any last-minute attempts to relieve them of their money by surrounding themselves with hired toughs. A couple of sly youths whistled their way nonchalantly down the avenue, trying to give the impression they were going anywhere but the bank.

As the grand silhouette of the old church appeared on the horizon, lights burning fiercely outside its high arched windows, Raquella tapped Harry on the shoulder.

"Well, we're here," she said. "I can't say I'm entirely clear as to what we do next, though."

"I was hoping you were going to tell me," Harry admitted. "You're Vendetta's maid, after all. Can't you just go in and tell them your master wants you to open one of the safety deposit boxes?"

Raquella shook her head. "I've never even been inside the bank. I'm his maid, not his secretary."

"That makes things a little bit complicated," replied Harry. He ransacked his pockets, producing a grubby pot-pourri of pencil shavings, boiled sweets and copper pennies. "Hmm . . . I doubt they'll let me buy a deposit box with this. How much have you got in your purse?"

"I used the last of *my* money getting us out of the poorhouse," Raquella replied evenly. "So don't look at me."

"Fair enough," Harry said. "We'll just have to make it up as we go along, then."

He banged on the roof of the carriage, and the coachman brought the cab to a halt outside the gabled entrance to the bank. Light was spilling out through the open door on to the street. As she stepped down on to the pavement, careful to avoid a murky puddle, Raquella saw that two gargoyles had been carved on either side of the doorway, their faces leering as they held out hands demanding payment. The cold night air sent a shiver down her spine.

"Hey!" the coachman called out after them indignantly. "This ain't a charity, you know! Where's my fare?"

"Call on Arthur Blake at the *Informer*," the boy shouted back. "Tell him Harry said you'd get a big tip."

He hustled Raquella away before the coachman could reply, shaking his head ruefully. "Arthur's going to kill me for that," Harry muttered. "He *hates* stumping up for expenses."

The maid wasn't listening; her attention was fixed on the doorway before her. In all her years of service, she had never once set foot inside the Bank of Darkside. Now, as she crossed the threshold, she was confronted with a sight of eerie beauty. There were still faint reminders of the building's previous incarnation as a church: a row of dusty organ pipes; the mosaic floor; the fluted columns that stretched up to a ceiling so high it was lost in shadow. Only now the stained-glass windows had been altered, their religious scenes replaced by dazzling piles of coins and treasure chests that bathed the church floor in a kaleidoscope of gold, silver and bronze colours. Where worshippers would once have congregated in the pews to hear sermons, clerks now sat at raised platforms, weighing out gold on sets of small scales and counting handfuls of notes. At the far end of the building, where the altar would once have taken pride of place, a figure was now presiding over a wooden desk weighed down with paperwork.

Darksiders were milling across the floor of the old nave, glancing suspiciously at one another as they kept their valuables close to their chests. The din was strangely muted, although it didn't mean that the queues were orderly. As Raquella watched, a one-legged man with a heavily scarred face elbowed past a young lady and slammed down a bag of coins on one of the platforms. The clerk eyed him wearily, but said nothing as he began to count the booty.

Harry let out a low whistle. "This wasn't what I was expecting."

"Amazing, isn't it?" Raquella breathed.

"Very atmospheric, but that's not quite what I meant. Where's the security? This is the biggest bank in Darkside, and I can't see any guards. There aren't even bars over the windows!"

The maid shook her head. "You're not looking properly," she said. "There's thousand of guards here. You just can't see them."

Harry frowned. "What – so they're invisible guards?"

"I can hear them," Raquella said softly. "I would recognize their sound anywhere."

Straining his ears, Harry could just make out a high-pitched sound above the sullen hubbub of the crowd. As he craned his neck upwards, the boy realized that the darkness up by the ceiling wasn't still, but was rippling and fluttering to the beating of a multitude of wings.

"Oh," Harry said, swallowing. "Bats."

"You could try and steal something from here," Raquella mused, "but how would you get out again?" There was a dreamlike look in her eyes as she surveyed the bank. "My father was meant to work here, many years ago, for Vendetta. Perhaps, if he had, then maybe I too. . ." Her voice trailed off, and she looked down at the floor.

Harry was searching for something to say when he caught sight of Hugo La Mort hastening through the crowd, his slicked-down hair gleaming in the soft lamplight. The doctor was making for the wooden desk at the back of the church.

"There he is," Harry said grimly. "Come on."

They hurried across the nave and began to fight their way through the crowds, ignoring the cries of protest and retaliatory elbows. Someone pushed Raquella in the back – Harry turned round to deal with her assailant, but the maid shouted at him to ignore it. Above the heads of the throng, he could see La Mort moving past the desk, and through a dark archway beyond. There wasn't a second to waste.

Once they had battled past the platforms, the crowds thinned. Harry raced up a set of steps and skidded to a halt in front of the desk. A small nameplate read "Mr Edmund Worsley – Head Clerk". The heavyset man in question had his head down and was engrossed in stamping a series of documents.

"Excuse me?" Harry said politely.

He started as Mr Worsley looked up. Vendetta's head clerk wasn't human. His oily, dark-grey skin gleamed in the candlelight, while his eyes were tiny and set far apart. Where a human's mouth would have been was instead a dripping maw filled with sharp, tiny teeth. Though he was wearing the normal garb of a Victorian clerk, the white cuffs and collar of his shirt were stained with an oozing green liquid. He was – Harry realized suddenly – a leech.

When Mr Worsley spoke, it was in a supple, squelching tone.

"Yes? And how may I help you, young sir?"

"Good question," Harry said, thinking frantically. "I have recently come into the possession of some family heirlooms and was thinking of storing them in one of your deposit boxes for safekeeping. However, these heirlooms are of great value to me, and first I want to be assured that they would be well-protected here."

Mr Worsley gave out a bubbling chuckle. "What a cautious young man you are. Well, I can assure you that we have had no complaints on that score."

"Even so," Harry said. "I'd like to see for myself. Would it be possible to tour the vaults?"

"Certainly," Mr Worsley replied. "If you could just show me your deposit box key, you can go straight down."

"But I've just told you I don't have one yet!"

The head clerk inhaled thickly. "Then I would presume our conversation is at an end, young man."

He returned to stamping his documents. Harry flashed Raquella a helpless look. The maid stepped forward and delicately cleared her throat.

"You do understand," she whispered, trying not to retch as she leaned near the leech's oozing skin, "the nature of the heirlooms we are talking about? This is the son of James Ripper – his possessions are more than mere trinkets and baubles. I would have thought that Mr Vendetta would welcome his custom."

The leech's eyes narrowed to slits. "Anyone can say they're a Ripper—"

"It would be sheer madness to impersonate a Ripper!" Raquella replied. "Do we look insane to you?"

Letting out a watery sigh, Mr Worsley nodded at the door behind him. "Follow the stairs. I'll be keeping an eye on you, mind."

Raquella smiled, elated, and followed Harry as he hastened through the archway and down a set of spiralling stone steps. It was colder here, cobwebs shuddering in the draughts. They headed deep beneath the earth before coming out in a low-vaulted room that ran underneath the floor of the bank. In the days of the church, it would have been a crypt, the lasting resting place of the faithful. But the remains had long since been removed, and only secrets were buried here now – stored in numbered, wrought-iron boxes that lined the wall like a square honeycomb. In the gloom, Raquella saw the outline of La Mort on the other side of the cellar. He was on his knees, cradling a box in his arms and cooing softly to himself.

Raquella barely saw Harry move. By the time the doctor had whirled around, it was too late; the boy was upon him. Harry struck a blow across the back of La Mort's head, sending the contents of his box spilling out over the floor with a silvery tinkle. Crying out in pain, the doctor made a desperate attempt to retrieve one of his items, only for Harry to stamp mercilessly on his hand. The boy fell on La Mort, pinning him to the ground with his knees. He raised his hand to strike the doctor again, only for Raquella to stay his hand. Harry's eyes flashed with anger.

"Enough," she said softly. "It is ended."

"The girl is right," a voice said behind them. They spun round, to see the hulking figure of Mr Worsley slithering down the steps of the crypt. La Mort wailed; whether in pain or fear, Raquella couldn't tell.

"For someone in Vendetta's service, you must think your master rather a stupid man," the head clerk continued as he approached. "We knew that something like this might happen. It is lucky for you that Vendetta made us aware of Miss Joubert's position. Do not think that you would have made it this far otherwise. We do not let any Tom, Dick or . . . Harry down to the vault."

Harry nodded at the prone form of La Mort. "What happens to him?"

"One cannot try to cross Vendetta and escape punishment," the leech replied slowly, slime dripping from his maw on to the crypt floor. "We will take the appropriate steps. There are other, deeper vaults in the bank – vaults where we will not be disturbed."

"*Non!*" La Mort gasped. "But you cannot mean. . ." He grabbed at Harry imploringly as Mr Worsley hauled him to his feet. "You cannot let them do this to me – you must help me, *mon ami*!"

"I'm no friend of yours," Harry shot back. "Frederick Longbourne sent me."

And with that, Harry turned his back on the doctor as he was dragged away, his screams echoing horribly around the vault. Harry bent over and picked up one of the silver items that had fallen from La Mort's deposit box.

A scalpel gleamed in the gloom.

"Surgical tools?" Harry said, his voice ringing with disbelief. "He went through all that just for *this*?"

"I suppose for La Mort, his instruments were the most important thing he owned," Raquella replied gently. "He told Jonathan that they were the finest set in Darkside. No wonder he'd try anything to get them back. Is there nothing else with them?"

The deposit box was still lying where it had fallen from La Mort's grasp. Peering into the bottom, Raquella saw that it was lined with official-looking documents. As Harry tossed the scalpel away with a sigh, she sat down on the floor and began leafing through them.

"What have you got there?" asked Harry, peering over her shoulder. "Anything interesting?"

"Not really," Raquella reported, lips pursed with

concentration. "Prescriptions, committals, charges—" She gasped suddenly. "Oh, Harry, no!"

"Raquella? What is it?"

The maid's face had turned a ghastly shade of pale. Her hands were trembling as she put down the document she was reading.

"We have to find Jonathan," she said. "Now."

24

A chill breeze sliced through the clearing, unsettling the trees that surrounded the grave of James Ripper and nagging at the clothes of the five figures congregated around it. Were it not for the late hour, the locked cemetery gates, and the atmosphere of fearful anticipation, they could have passed for mourners paying their last respects. As it was, they looked more like gravediggers – which was perhaps closer to the truth.

This wasn't at all what Jonathan had expected. He had imagined that a member of Darkside's first family would have been buried in an ornate tomb or a grand mausoleum, not this simple, almost apologetic mound of earth hidden away at the back of a north London cemetery. There wasn't even a headstone above the grave, no clue to the identity of the man who lay here.

"James died before the Succession," Vendetta said, answering the unspoken question hanging in the air. "There is a certain amount of shame involved in that."

"It wasn't his fault!" Jonathan protested. "He was ambushed by his own brother!"

"Even so," the vampire replied. "He was a Ripper. They have their own code."

Compared to everyone else in the clearing, Vendetta was a study in icy calm. Josiah Bartlemas was hopping from one foot to the other, barely able to contain his excitement, while Kate looked pale and shell-shocked – although, given her recent traumas, Jonathan was amazed she was still standing upright. But it was Carnegie's demeanour that troubled him. Usually Jonathan knew exactly what to expect from his ally, but the wereman had been a strangely compliant figure all evening. Knowing Vendetta's plan – and the blood he needed to drain for James's resurrection – Jonathan had expected Carnegie to explode at any second. Yet the wereman had kept a subdued distance, not once threatening trouble.

The more Jonathan thought about it, the more he wondered whether Carnegie actually wanted Vendetta to succeed. Although the wereman had saved Jonathan's life time and time again, each occasion had brought him into conflict with both Lucien and Marianne. Whichever of the living Rippers won the Succession, what sort of life lay in store for Elias Carnegie afterwards? Would James's return offer him a priceless second chance? This time, would Carnegie stand by and leave Jonathan at Vendetta's mercy?

With a grand flourish, Bartlemas produced the Chronos Wheel from his pocket. The mechanism had been coated in moonstone, the white mineral glowing with a pale luminescence. As the watchmaker hunched down by the graveside, making final adjustments to the Wheel's settings, Vendetta glanced from Kate to Jonathan, thoughtfully tapping his cheek with the barrel of his pistol.

"So, I did promise to choose which one of you will be assisting Bartlemas tonight. It's not an easy decision, I must confess. Hmm. . ."

One glance at Kate's wan features was enough for Jonathan. He stepped forward.

"Enough. Use my blood."

Vendetta arched an eyebrow. "Volunteering, Jonathan? How very heroic of you."

"Step back, boy," Carnegie barked. "You're not doing this."

Jonathan turned and gave the wereman a resolute look. "Yes, I am. It's either me or Kate, and she's been through enough."

"I'm not just going to stand here and watch them kill you."

"The boy may not *necessarily* die," Bartlemas murmured, glancing up at the stars. "If the resurrection progresses smoothly, there is a small chance he could be left with enough blood to survive."

"But feel free to step in at any time," Vendetta said, pointedly holding up his pistol.

"You think that pop-gun will stop me?" Carnegie growled.

"Perhaps not." In a smooth movement Vendetta turned

away from the wereman and trained the weapon on Jonathan. "But then, I won't be firing it at you. Make one move," the vampire continued, "and I'll shoot the boy through the heart. And then he'll most certainly die."

"If he does," the wereman rumbled back, "you won't leave this clearing alive."

There was a tense pause, and then Jonathan said finally: "It's all right, Carnegie, really. There's no other way."

He patted the wereman on the arm and nodded at Kate, who gave him a trembling smile in return. Though he was trying to appear bullish, Jonathan couldn't ignore the thundering of his heart and the tightness in his chest as he took his place beside Bartlemas. With one hand the watchmaker rolled up Jonathan's sleeve, whilst placing the Chronos Wheel beneath the boy's arm with the other.

"You should be honoured!" he whispered. "You get to complete my family's great work – your name will become legend!"

Looking into Bartlemas's wild eyes, Jonathan saw that the last grains of sanity were falling away – the watchmaker had become totally consumed by his quest. Before he could raise a protest, Bartlemas gripped him tightly by the arm, and slashed a knife across his skin. Jonathan felt a sharp pain, and then blood came spurting out from his vein. Unable to watch as the life streamed out of him down on to the Wheel, Jonathan gazed defiantly at Vendetta, willing the vampire to make a sharp comment. Vendetta stared coolly back, but said nothing, his gun still pointedly levelled.

There was a soft whirring sound as the mechanism clicked into life, and the cogs of the Chronos Wheel began to revolve around the tiny metal sphere.

"It has begun," Bartlemas hissed in his ear.

At the sound of a regular ticking noise, the wind picked up in the clearing, sending dead leaves skittering across the ground in a vast spiral around James's grave.

"It is working!" Vendetta proclaimed excitedly. "It is working!"

The cogs began to turn faster and faster, until the clicks formed one continuous humming sound. Triumphantly crying out his grandfather's name, Bartlemas exhorted the Wheel to spin faster and faster. The watchmaker was keeping tight hold of Jonathan, who was already feeling woozy from blood loss. As the boy swayed, Carnegie took a step forward, only for Vendetta to halt him with a wave of his pistol.

There was a deep rumbling sound from beneath the ground, and then suddenly a jet of earth erupted from James's grave and into the air like lava from a volcano, covering Jonathan and Bartlemas in soil. As his blood continued to run over the Wheel, Jonathan cried out in agony, but the sound was swallowed up by the howling wind. His legs were going numb, and were it not for Bartlemas's iron grip he would have been buffeted to the ground. The earth in James's grave began to spin in a giant whirlpool, circling with such ferocity that it threatened to drag them all into its clutches. Through the churning soil, Jonathan saw a hand break through the surface, fingers yearning for the night air.

"He is rising!" Vendetta shouted above the clamour.

There came a sharp report from somewhere in the trees, and Bartlemas screamed. The watchmaker staggered forward clutching his chest, his cherished creation slipping from his hands. There was another report, and Vendetta threw himself to one side. With the link between himself and the Chronos Wheel brutally severed, Jonathan felt his legs give way beneath him, and heard Kate scream. As he fell to the ground, his mind spiralling into a deep black hole, Jonathan heard gunfire.

Jonathan reeled in and out of consciousness, unsure where his dreams ended and reality began. Men were shouting; they were voices he didn't recognize. Carnegie roared back a challenge. The sound of gunshots echoed around the clearing. A face appeared in Jonathan's mind: a young, handsome face with blond hair and cold eyes. The expression on his face was indecipherable as he mouthed the word "farewell".

Suddenly everything went quiet.

"Jonathan?" a voice asked urgently near his ear.

Stirring, he realized that Kate was kneeling beside him. The girl had torn off a strip of material from somewhere, and was tying a tourniquet around his bloodstained arm.

"Are you OK?" she whispered, her eyes alive with fright.

Jonathan laughed weakly, nodding. "Just great," he said, slurring slightly.

"You have to get up now," she said.

"'M tired," Jonathan replied. "Gonna lie here."

"You'll get up now," a voice boomed.

Jonathan looked up.

The clearing looked as though a tornado had ripped through it. James's grave had exploded, scattering dark earth across the grass, but there was no sign of the corpse that had lain there. Next to Jonathan, Bartlemas's body was sprawled out over the ground. The Chronos Wheel lay on the ground near him, just beyond the watchmaker's outstretched hand. It had shattered in a thousand pieces. At the edge of the clearing, men were training guns at Jonathan, arranged in a row like a firing squad. Although they were dressed in Darkside suits and top hats, they were carrying some very modern-looking weaponry. In between them stood Elias Carnegie. Pinned down by the guns, the wereman was twitching with frustration.

As Kate helped Jonathan climb woozily to his feet, he realized that there was another man in the clearing, standing just behind the row of gunmen. A long cloak failed to mask his broad shoulders. He threw back the cowl of his hood, revealing a shock of white hair. It was the man Jonathan had seen outside Bartlemas's shop: Holborn, the Abettor of Darkside. A look of utter contempt was slashed across his features.

"I must congratulate you on your efforts," he said sonorously, making a sweeping gesture across the battered remains of the clearing. "The watchmaker is dead. Vendetta has fled like a coward into the night. James Ripper's rest has been brutally disturbed. And all for nothing."

"Where did the body go?" Jonathan asked, looking at the empty grave in a daze.

"That is a question beyond the comprehension of us all," Holborn replied. "A lesson to you, perhaps, not to meddle with powers you cannot possibly understand."

"You were watching us," Carnegie said flatly. "You'd been waiting for us all along."

"Well, obviously," Holborn snorted. "Vendetta is losing his touch. Did he think that Thomas could make all those payments to Bartlemas without my knowledge? I knew of their little scheme, their foolish dreams of bringing James back. A half-wit could have anticipated Vendetta's appearance here. Now he has been stopped, the Blood Succession will take place tonight. Lucien is travelling to Battersea Power Station as we speak, where he will face his sister. Sadly, you will not be there to see it. It will be a glorious victory, I guarantee."

"You surprise me, Holborn," Carnegie said. "Rumour had it that you'd do anything for power, but I never thought you'd align yourself with such lowlife. I wonder what Thomas would have made of you siding with James's killer."

Holborn's face broke into a sneer. "I care little for what that decrepit old fool thought. While he curled up in his bed and wasted away, I ran Darkside." His voice swept majestically through the clearing. "I was more than an Abettor – I was the Ripper myself!"

"You're a fool," the wereman said, bluntly breaking the

spell of Holborn's oratory. "Do you think Lucien's going to share the throne with you? Once he's in power you'll be thrown in the deepest dungeon in Blackchapel."

"Perhaps," Holborn replied. "Perhaps I won't share power with him. One way or another, it will hardly be of your concern."

Throwing his hood back over his white hair, the Abettor walked out of the clearing, giving his men a final command as he left.

"Kill them. Now."

25

As Holborn melted into the trees, time seemed to freeze before Jonathan's eyes. He watched in torturous slow motion as the gunmen raised their weapons and took aim. Carnegie responded by throwing his head back and roaring as he started to transform, the hackles on his neck rising and bulging, but there was no way the wereman could reach the gunmen in time to stop them firing. Jonathan knew that he should try and run for cover, but he was too tired and weak to feel scared. In the endless second that followed, he simply gave Kate's hand a squeeze, and waited for shots to ring out.

One of the gunmen screamed.

It was a sound Jonathan would never forget, a high-pitched squeal of agony and terror that he would never have thought a man's vocal chords capable of making. The gunman on the far left of the line had dropped his weapon and was writhing in the shadows, clutching at his neck. As everyone in the clearing paused, united in shock, Jonathan saw that something had attacked the man from behind. Even as he watched, dumbfounded, a dagger gleamed devilishly in the darkness, and the screams were abruptly silenced.

Regaining their senses, the remaining gunmen whirled round and began blasting away into the trees, but their assailant was already upon them. The knife gleamed again, and another gunman was stopped in his tracks; another was felled by an unseen blow. Jonathan had witnessed several of Darkside's most brutally effective fighters at work, but had never seen such a deathly quiet, unanswerable killer. He suddenly realized that it could only be one man – dumbfounded, Jonathan watched as Vendetta wove a delicate web of death.

With the gunmen diverted, Carnegie waded howling into the fray, knocking the nearest man unconscious with a shuddering uppercut, and falling on to his neighbour before he had a chance to target his weapon. Beset on both sides, the gunmen panicked: Jonathan pulled Kate down to the ground as bullets began spraying over their heads. When the shooting finally stopped, Jonathan saw the last gunman fleeing away through the trees, Vendetta hot on his heels.

At that moment a resplendent full moon sprang out from behind a cloudbank, bathing the clearing in milky white light. Carnegie barked several times, stretching out his limbs as he felt the moonlight on his fur.

With the danger seemingly over, Jonathan gingerly rose to his feet, helping Kate up with him.

"Be careful," he warned. "Carnegie's not safe when's he like this."

As Kate nodded stoically, Jonathan wondered whether anything could surprise her again after this night. Though they cautiously backed away from the wereman, Carnegie seemed unaware of their presence. Instead he prowled amongst the bodies littering the grass, his shoulders still taut with violence, a low growl emanating from his throat.

"What's he doing?" Kate murmured.

"I'm not sure," Jonathan replied. "But I don't like the look of it."

Following the rough direction of Carnegie's gaze, they peered into the trees. There, picked out in the moonlight, Jonathan saw the silhouette of two figures locked together in a close embrace: the last gunman and Vendetta. Still giddy from blood loss, at first Jonathan thought that they were dancing, but then he saw that the gunman's legs were shaking violently, and there was a bubbling sound coming from his mouth, as though he were drowning. When the vampire released him, the man collapsed to the floor like a rag doll.

The silhouette paused, drawing an arm across its mouth, and then Vendetta strode back into the clearing. His cool, handsome face had metamorphosed into the angular, hate-filled features of a vampire: dead eyes set into yellowed, leathery skin. Two long fangs protruded from his mouth, which was streaked with blood.

Carnegie snarled, and it was then, in the moonlit

graveyard, that Jonathan saw the wereman and the vampire confront one another in their true, bestial forms.

"You ran away," Carnegie rumbled.

The vampire ran a long, thick tongue over his stained fangs. "It was a trap. I had to turn the odds in my favour. Be thankful I returned at all, wolfman, and that there are others I detest more than you."

"You missed Holborn."

Vendetta inclined his head. "There will be other opportunities."

"So what now?"

The wereman was still coiled like a spring. Jonathan was all too aware that under the influence of the full moon, the beast within Carnegie would be straining to attack, regardless of the opponent – that the blood lust running through his veins would always demand more carnage.

Vendetta looked around at the strewn bodies. "Now, I feed."

"There's no time!" Jonathan cried out.

Their stand-off interrupted, the creatures turned and glared at him, united in violence and hatred. As Kate took an instinctive step backwards, Jonathan was suddenly acutely aware that the danger hadn't abated.

"You heard Holborn!" he persisted. "The Blood Succession is happening tonight! We've got to go to Battersea and stop Lucien!"

"*We* won't be doing anything," the vampire hissed. "You

should just be grateful you have a chance of leaving this clearing alive."

"Forget about me!" Jonathan cried. "If Marianne dies, Lucien will become the new Ripper. What will you do then?"

"Holborn leaves little to chance, Starling. Marianne was as good as dead the moment her father passed away. You will forgive me if I save my tears. There is bloodshed ahead, and I need to plan my next move. Trying to intervene now would be foolish beyond measure."

"But. . .!"

"Shut up, boy." Carnegie's voice was a guttural rumble. He pointed a long finger at Jonathan. "Save your speeches. You don't know what you're talking about. What do you know about Darkside? About the Rippers?" The wereman's claws glinted in the moonlight as he loomed closer. "About *hunger*?"

Seeing the complete absence of humanity in Carnegie's eyes, it took all of Jonathan's self-control not to turn on his heel and run. Instead, he drew himself up and held the wereman's gaze.

"You agree with the vampire, then? We sit here and do nothing, give Lucien the throne?"

For a second it looked as though Carnegie was going to lunge at him. Then the wereman broke off, muttering to himself. He sank to his haunches, scratching at his fur as though he were crawling with insects.

Kate clutched at Jonathan. "We should go. He doesn't look like he wants us here."

"It's not Carnegie's fault," Jonathan replied edgily. "It's the full moon. He's trying to fight it."

"Get out of here," the wereman said, through clenched teeth. "I can't hold back much longer."

"But what am I going to do?"

"RUN, boy!"

Grabbing Kate's hand, Jonathan sprinted out of the clearing and back along the winding overgrown path, branches and thorns snagging his clothing and tearing at his skin. As they exploded out of the undergrowth and back on to the broad promenade that led out of the cemetery, an anguished howl echoed around the gravestones behind them.

It wasn't until they had raced out through the cemetery gates that Jonathan skidded to a breathless halt. Behind him, the graveyard had once more descended into silence – there was no sign of Carnegie. Jonathan swore angrily to himself, a mixture of tiredness and frustration welling up within him. Not only had his closest ally come within an inch of attacking him, but now Jonathan had to try and stop Lucien on his own. It seemed an impossible task.

Determined to put that thought out of his mind, he began walking briskly down the road.

"Jonathan, wait!" Kate called out. "Where are you going?"

"Battersea."

She raced after him, forcing him to pull up. "But that's crazy! Vendetta said it was hopeless, and he's a vampire, for heaven's sake! Even if you hadn't lost all that blood, what do you think you can do in Battersea, besides get yourself killed?"

"I don't know," he replied stubbornly, folding his arms. "I'll work it out when I get there."

"I know you want to do something," Kate said, more softly this time. "But you're in no state to do anything now. I mean, look at your arm."

Jonathan glanced down at it. The bandage was soaked with dark red liquid, and his fingers were tingling.

"Come on," she continued gently, "at least get someone to look at it."

It was so tempting to give in – part of Jonathan knew that she was right. Even so, he shook his head.

"I can't. This isn't just about the Blood Succession for me. Lucien's the only person who knows what happened to my mum, and if there's the smallest chance I can find out from him, I have to take it. After tonight I might never get another chance." He paused. "You could come with me, you know."

Kate stared up into the night sky, gazing at the full moon. Then it was her turn to shake her head. "I'm sorry. I want to help you, I do, but . . . it's just that *my* mum's sitting at home with my dad and they'll be going mad with worry. I've got to let them know I'm all right. And maybe now I know about Darkside, I can get them to stop arguing all the time. I can't miss that chance either. Do you understand?"

"Yeah." Jonathan nodded. "I do."

He gave her a quick hug, and then jokingly wagged a

finger at her. "Whatever happens, remember you're a half-Darkside now. Don't go giving us a bad name."

"No, Jonathan," Kate replied with a smile. "*You're* a half-Darksider. I'm a half-Lightsider. That's the difference between me and you."

He grinned wryly. "I guess so. Good luck."

Kate gave him a serious smile, and then reached up and kissed him on the cheek. "Keep it," she whispered. "You're going to need it more than me."

They parted by the steps that led down to Archway tube station. As he watched Kate climb wearily aboard her bus home, Jonathan nearly called out after her, knowing that there was more he wanted to say to her. But he knew Kate was right – she needed to go back to her family and let them know she was alive. Jonathan watched silently as the bus drove out of sight before he turned and hastened down the station steps.

By now it was late evening, and the Underground was quiet. Jonathan sat in the carriage at the back of the train, his sleeve rolled over the bloodstained bandage. Still weakened from the blood loss, he lolled in his seat like a drunkard, drifting in and out of consciousness. Needing to change lines at Euston, he sleepwalked through the station, barely in control of his own footsteps, grateful that his Lightside anonymity shielded him from the inspection of other passengers.

It was getting harder to be sure where he was. As the

train clattered through the tunnels to a rhythmic beat, Jonathan felt cobblestones beneath him, heard horses whinnying as he raced a carriage through the streets of Darkside. When a group of loud teenagers got on his carriage, shouting and playing music on their mobile phones, he imagined himself at a lavish party in the Cain Club, where masked revellers draped an arm across his shoulder and toasted his health.

But throughout these dreams, there was one constant, shadowy presence: Lucien. Even as Jonathan was engulfed by the urge for revenge, he could almost feel the Ripper's anticipation. After all, there was the promise of death in the air tonight.

26

On a high iron walkway at the top of Battersea Power Station, Sergeant Charlie Wilson leaned over the rail and stared down into the exposed innards of the building. Disused for decades, the power station was a scarred husk. The roof had been ripped away and the floors knocked through, creating a vast enclosed space: the perfect arena, in fact, for a fight to the death.

The building was situated in the middle of a patch of scruffy wasteland, cordoned off from the public by a high security fence on the south side and the River Thames on the north. Behind Wilson, two railway tracks snaked round the side of the building before coming together at Grosvenor Bridge. He was facing east, high enough not only for a panoramic view of London but also for the biting wind to make the walkway an exposed, precarious place. At each corner of the power station, a giant chimney rose into the sky, its base encased in scaffolding.

Wilson had spent the days following his visit to

Blackchapel frantically preparing for the Blood Succession. In a deserted warehouse in south London, he was introduced to a gang of Darksiders Holborn had sent over for support. In his brief career, the young sergeant had never seen such a bunch of criminal lowlifes: petty thieves and pickpockets; battle-scarred humans and grotesque creatures. Half of them were suffering from the after-effects of crossing, and were sprawled out on the warehouse floor, groaning and clutching at their stomachs. When they eventually picked themselves up, Wilson was charged with the unenviable task of introducing the gang to modern weapons, and for two consecutive nights the building had echoed with the sound of cackling laughter and wild gunfire. Watching the Darksiders pepper the walls with bullets, Wilson couldn't help but wonder whether these were the sort of men a policeman should be training. As ever, Carmichael batted away his questions with enigmatic replies.

The hunchbacked detective had been busy, too – pulling strings to replace the round-the-clock security that protected the power station with some slightly more amenable guards. As Wilson and Carmichael had driven through the gates earlier that evening, two heavyset Darksiders had ushered them through, their porcine eyes scanning the road beyond for unwelcome guests. The two detectives had clambered up a ladder to their lofty position, the hunchback grunting with the effort. Flaming torches had been placed at intervals along the walls, draping the station in a ghostly illumination.

"Isn't someone going to notice all this?' Wilson puffed.

"They can notice all they want," the detective replied. "I've told the top brass that we're conducting a training exercise here tonight. No one's going to bother us."

Now there came the clank of footsteps on the iron walkway, and Holborn strode purposefully towards them. Carmichael looked up and raised an inquisitive eyebrow. The Abettor nodded.

"It has been taken care of," he said.

"A pity," Carmichael mused. "I rather liked the Starling boy."

"He brought it on himself. There was no alternative."

Wilson frowned. The name Starling sounded familiar. "You're not talking about the lad we interviewed for the Kensington robbery, are you? What's he got to do with this?"

"Nothing. Now," Holborn said pointedly.

"What do you mean? What did you do to him? You didn't. . .?"

The Abettor said nothing, merely raised a white eyebrow.

Wilson grabbed Carmichael's arm. "Listen, boss, I know that keeping Darkside a secret is important, but you can't go around killing kids! That's crazy!"

"Not now, Wilson!" Carmichael snapped. It was the first time Wilson had ever heard the hunchback raise his voice. He turned to Holborn. "My apologies, Abettor. Ignore him. Where is Lucien?"

"He is preparing in private. This night will take much out of him. Remember that he can only maintain the form of the Black Phoenix for so long."

"That's not going to be a problem," Carmichael said. "This place is crawling with our men. If Lucien fails to take care of her as the Phoenix, we'll be ready to step in. Marianne will get shot full of holes before she takes as much as a step towards him."

"You might as well shoot her in the back now and be done with it," Wilson said glumly.

"Charlie!" the hunchback replied, in mock surprise. "This is the Blood Succession! There's got to be at least a semblance of a contest."

"And then we'll shoot her," Holborn added.

A red-faced Darksider came running up towards them, throwing a messy approximation of a salute. "You asked to see me, sir?"

"Is everything secure?" Holborn asked crisply.

"We've had men stationed all around the perimeter fence for five hours, sir. They're reporting anything that moves. As soon as Marianne tries to get into the power station, you'll know about it."

"Is that so?" Carmichael said thoughtfully, looking down at the ground. "Then who on Darkside is that?"

Getting in had been easy. Not for first time in her life, Marianne had cause to be grateful for her special perfume's distracting qualities. With its spicy aroma hanging in the air, it had been a simple matter to slip past the dopey guards on the gate and into the power station. Marianne had no idea what to expect inside, but there was no way she was going to announce her presence.

She was dressed in simple soldier's garb: trousers and boots, a shirt. Her hair was dyed blood red, save for one black lock. She pushed it behind her ear as she examined her surroundings with a calculating, military eye. Peering up into the night sky, she picked out the figures standing on the highest walkway. It didn't matter who they were – tonight, Marianne was treating everyone as a potential threat. Mentally marking their position, she continued her surveillance, noting the lower walkways running along the wall that could provide shelter from the attacks of the Black Phoenix. Lucien would come at her from the air, hoping to kill her quickly before he reverted back to his fragile human form. If she stayed out in the open, she'd play right into his hands. However, if Marianne could survive the initial onslaught, finishing him off would be a simple matter.

It was a big *if*, she knew. Her previous encounters with the Phoenix at Greenwich and in the Cain Club had been enough to convince Marianne that she faced an awesomely powerful creature. After all, it had ended James's life, and all of Darkside knew of his reputation as a fighter. There was a good chance she would die here tonight. Perhaps she should have been scared, but then, Marianne couldn't remember the last time she had felt fear. Even as a child, she had never cried or wailed. Now the only thing she felt was a tidal wave of adrenaline and the icy excitement of an impending battle.

Marianne drew her long sword, the blade making a metallic zinging sound as it was freed from its scabbard. The bounty hunter felt reassured by the balance of the weapon, and the weight of it in her hand. She shifted her feet, adopting a wider, braced stance, and waited for her brother to try to kill her.

"But how did she. . .?" the guard spluttered. "I swear, sir, there's no way she could have got past us!"

"And yet here she is," Holborn said darkly. "We'll discuss this later. What I want to know is – where are Humble and Skeet?"

"Marianne's men," Carmichael explained to Wilson in a whisper. "She never travels without them."

"I don't want any more surprises," the Abettor said. "Find them. Now."

The guard scurried off into the darkness, leaving the three men alone on the gantry. Holborn descended into a moody reverie, while Carmichael stared out at the twinkling lights of the city centre across the Thames, lost in thought. Unwilling to disturb the silence, Wilson watched Marianne calmly wait for Lucien. She stood as still as a statue, sword drawn and levelled. It was an impressive display of self-control. Once again, the young detective had cause to doubt whether he was on the right side.

After ten minutes the guard reappeared, red-faced and out of breath.

"Humble and Skeet aren't here, sir."

The Abettor grabbed hold of the guard's shirt with a large fist. "Are you sure?"

"We've scoured the entire area, sir," the guard replied. "She's come alone."

Holborn looked down at the lone woman standing in the centre of the arena, and broke into rich, baritone laughter.

"I don't believe it!" he said. "She's playing *fair*!"

Jonathan disembarked from the tube train at Pimlico and followed the sparse crowd of people to the exit. Dazed from blood loss, on the escalator out of the station, he nearly fell backwards into the man standing behind him. Jonathan smelled alcohol, and heard the man laugh harshly.

"Bit young to be drinking, aren't you?" he said. "You look like you've had more than me."

Jonathan mumbled a reply and staggered out of the station. He paused on the street, the fresh air clearing his head a little, then made his way down a broad avenue towards the riverfront. Battersea Power Station loomed over the other side of the Thames, the outline of two large cranes standing idly by. Jonathan wasn't sure how long it took him to cross the bridge and find himself on the desolate road that ran around the back of the power station. In bright sunshine the area would have looked bleak; in the clutches of midnight, it was downright forbidding.

A fence of tall wooden boards ran around the back of the building, beneath signs warning against trespassing. They were too high to scramble over, but at one point they gave way to a slightly lower brick wall that, if he stood on his tiptoes, Jonathan could just about see over. Gritting his teeth, he placed his hands on top of the wall and hauled himself up, ignoring the pain in his damaged wrist. He expended so much energy getting over that he fell down the other side, landing with a thump on the hard ground.

Now Jonathan was inside the grounds, he could see lights flickering inside the power station. There was no sound. For the first time since he had left the cemetery, he felt a twinge of uncertainty. He had reached the site of the Blood Succession – what was he going to do now?

A chill ran down the back of his spine, and Jonathan shivered uncontrollably. Looking up into the sky, he saw something moving through the darkness above the power station. Summoning his last reserves of energy, Jonathan broke into a shambling run across the scraggy wasteland. He was halfway to the power station when a shape reared up in front of him, and his head exploded with pain.

The Black Phoenix flew through the night sky towards the power station, powerful wings propelling it easily through the air. In this form, it felt nothing but hatred – its talons itching for the feel of human skin, its beak for the taste of warm blood. Circling around the power station, its sharp

27

Marianne tensed as the black cloud fell upon her, then sprang into the air to meet the Phoenix's dive. Screaming a battle cry at the top of her lungs, she blocked the thrust of the bird's beak, sparks flying from her sword. Absorbing the shuddering impact of the collision in her shoulder, she fell away to the Phoenix's left, dodging the wicked swipe of its talons. Hitting the ground, she shifted smoothly into a forward roll, and was back on her feet in seconds.

Although the black fog around her was absolute, since she'd fought Lucien before, Marianne was prepared. She had spent the previous week sparring blindfolded with Humble, and had become accustomed to fighting without the power of sight. The bounty hunter fell back on her other senses: heard the sound of beating wings as the bird dived in to attack, smelled the rotting flesh on its beak as it snapped at her. But more than that was an intuition formed from years of combat – an almost logical understanding of the pattern of blows and strikes that made up a fight, the steps that formed this dangerous dance. Parrying another talon assault, Marianne ducked instinctively as one of the Phoenix's leathery wings passed over her head.

As the bird came at her again, the bounty hunter reached down to the ground and picked up a handful of dirt, flinging it in its face. The Phoenix screeched as the powder stung its eyes. It was a cheap ploy worthy of a bar-room brawl, but Marianne didn't care. Anything to buy her time. For a minute both brother and sister fought blindly, frantically exchanging cuts and blows. Then the bird cawed with a mixture of triumph and blood lust and redoubled its attack.

As the black cloud bore down upon her, Marianne decided on a new tactic, standing firm until the last second, when she sidestepped like a matador. Although the bird shot past her, she hadn't moved far enough to prevent a long talon raking down her back. Grimacing with pain, Marianne reversed the grip on her sword and aimed a backhanded slice at the Phoenix's ribcage as it flew past. With grim satisfaction she heard the bird shriek in pain, and the cloud around it shuddered.

It was time for the real fighting to begin.

"Here," Carmichael said, passing Wilson a pair of high-tech goggles. "You'll need these."

The young sergeant said nothing as he strapped the night-vision goggles over his eyes. He hadn't seen the Black

Phoenix as it arrowed past them, but the torches beneath them had been suddenly extinguished, and an icy draught of fear struck Wilson's very core. Deluged by feelings of loss and loneliness, he suddenly felt very young.

Wilson flicked on the goggles, and his world descended into a fuzzy green, as though he were at the bottom of a deep swamp. Now he could see the battle taking place beneath him. Wilson shivered at the sight of the Phoenix – it was a giant black bird, so large that it seemed to have flown straight from the pages of mythology. Sleek and powerful, it should have been beautiful, but its wings were leathery like a bat, with thick veins pulsing along their length, and there was an all-pervasive atmosphere of malevolence around it, more powerful than any darkness. As it hovered above its opponent, unleashing a rain of vicious swipes on her, Wilson wondered how on earth anyone could hope to match it.

And yet, impossibly, Marianne *was* matching it. The bounty hunter moved with a deadly elegance, her sword weaving elaborate traces as she parried and thrusted with a speed that defied belief. Wilson's experience of armed combat had been limited to martial arts and action films; seeing this woman fight now, he realized how little he understood. Even as he watched, Marianne launched a counter-attack against the Phoenix, hurling a dagger from a sheath on her back and following it up with a flurry of sword strokes.

But for all Marianne's skill and bravery, even Wilson

could see that the woman was suffering. She was hobbling on her left leg, and the back of her shirt was in tatters where a long claw had raked it. It was only a matter of time. Wasn't it?

"It's closer than I thought it would be," Carmichael remarked in a neutral tone of voice as he adjusted his goggles. "Do you think we should intervene?"

The Abettor was engrossed in the battle, a slight smile playing across his lips. He shook his head.

"Let them play a while longer," he said.

Wilson saw his superior glance quickly at Holborn, but his expression was hidden behind the large goggles. Carmichael looked like he was going to say something, but then turned back to watch the battle.

Marianne could feel the fight slipping away from her. The Phoenix attacked without remorse, apparently unaffected by the two deep cuts across its ribcage and the blood gushing from a vein on its right wing. How long could this monstrosity maintain its form? Marianne had badly twisted her left knee, hampering her movement, and her wounds were beginning to take their toll. Her cheek was bleeding; she wasn't even sure how she had picked up the wound.

She desperately needed time to regroup. Once more her eyes flicked up to the walkways running along the east and west sides of the power station. Marianne began to back away from the Black Phoenix towards the east wall, maintaining a shield of defensive strokes. Then, feinting a counter-attack in one direction, the bounty hunter leapt backwards in the other, seeking the shelter of the lowest walkway.

The Black Phoenix hadn't been fooled. There was a rush of air, and a vast wing hit Marianne in mid-leap, knocking the sword from her grasp and sending her into a crumpled heap on to the floor of the power station.

The first thing Jonathan was aware of was a crashing pain in his temple. He opened his eyes to see a man standing over him, raising a rifle butt over his head.

"Lucky you took me by surprise," the man said conversationally. "Otherwise I'd have filled you full of holes."

"Don't . . . shoot," Jonathan muttered.

"Didn't you see the sign, sonny? No trespassers. Especially not tonight."

There was movement to Jonathan's left, and then another man appeared, casually balancing a gun over his shoulder as though it were a fishing rod. He peered at the boy on the ground.

"What've you got here, Ignatius?"

"A mouse," Ignatius replied. "I caught it scampering off towards the power station."

"Well, you know what to do with vermin," the new man said. "Shoot it."

"It's only a little mouse, Casper. Is it worth a bullet?"

"One, perhaps. Just make sure you don't miss."

"From this distance?" Ignatius scoffed. "Watch how a real marksman does it."

As the Darksider took aim, Jonathan snaked out a leg and kicked Ignatius hard in the kneecap. Caught off guard, the man fell over. Casper howled with laughter.

"You've got guts, lad, I'll give you that." He cast a pitying glance at Ignatius, who was trying to pick himself up in a dignified fashion. "However, you're still in the wrong place at the wrong time."

Casper brought his gun down from his shoulder and readied to fire. Jonathan was preparing for the end when there came an enraged howl from behind him, and then a familiar figure crashed into the fray.

Carmichael's head snapped upwards at the sound of the beast's cry. He looked out over the south wall to the wasteland behind the power station. Through his night-vision goggles, Wilson could just make out a group of figures wrestling on the ground.

"What's going on down there, sir?"

"Not sure," Carmichael replied. "But we need to find out. I'm not sure how much I trust our 'guards'."

"Shouldn't we stay here?"

The detective glanced down at Marianne's prostrate body. "It's over. Come on."

Strangely unwilling to leave, Wilson allowed himself to be led away along the walkway. Holborn didn't move a muscle as they passed by; the Abettor's eyes remained gleefully transfixed on the scene below him as he awaited the killing blow.

Chaos reigned in the grounds of Battersea Power Station. Shouts of alarm and confusion rang out into the night. Ignatius and Casper were now sprawled at Jonathan's feet, and by his side Elias Carnegie was flexing his claws.

"Carnegie!" Jonathan cried with relief. "What are you doing here?"

The wereman was looking in all directions, sizing up the situation. There were men racing at them from all sides of the wasteland, the first wild spray of bullets flying hopelessly into the air.

"No time to explain," Carnegie barked. "I'll distract the guards – you go and help Marianne."

The ring was tightening around them: ten, maybe twenty guards.

"There's too many!" Jonathan shouted. "And they've got guns! They'll kill you!"

"If Lucien wins, it doesn't matter," the wereman retorted. "We're all dead. You were right, boy. Now go!"

"I'm not going to leave you!"

"Go!" Carnegie snarled, pushing Jonathan away. He bayed one final time at the moon, and then bounded towards the nearest group of guards, avoiding their scattergun fire. The guards took the bait, ignoring the boy as they veered in on the wereman. As Jonathan hared towards the power station, he saw two figures hastening past him in the opposite direction. He heard a commanding voice shout out, "Take him alive! That's an order!"

Although part of Jonathan couldn't bear to look, he couldn't help glancing over his shoulder as he ran. Carnegie had downed at least three men, and was holding another by the throat, daring the other guards to try and shoot him. As the circle tightened around him, Jonathan saw someone hurl a giant net over the wereman, who raged and howled with anger. The guards closed in warily, and then brought down a hail of rifle butts on Carnegie until he sank to his knees and collapsed.

"NO!" Jonathan screamed.

He stopped, his heart torn. Although desperate to save his old friend, deep down Jonathan knew it was hopeless – he was too far away, facing too many guards. Remembering Carnegie's last words, Jonathan turned his back on the wereman and ran towards the power station, his eyes blinded by tears. But by then it was far too late.

As the Black Phoenix rose into the sky for its final, triumphant pass, Marianne knew that she was going to die. Her breath was coming in paltry wheezes, and her left arm was broken. Her sword lay far beyond her reach, snapped into two pieces by the sheer power of the Phoenix. She was bleeding from innumerable scratches and cuts. In many ways, it was a miracle she had avoided the killing blow for this long. Lucien – and, although he had assumed the form of this foul creature, she had never forgotten that it was her brother who had injured her in this way – cawed loudly, seemingly stronger than ever.

Even now, she felt no fear. She had heard that people facing death saw their life flash before their eyes, but Marianne indulged no such memories. Although her body was broken, her mind was still racing, calculating. She had one last card to play: a plan she had drawn up days before, which combined the best of Darkside thinking with Lightside technology. It would spell the end for her, but at least it would give her the eternal satisfaction of taking her accursed brother with her.

It was time. The Phoenix spread its wings and the cloak of darkness vanished – Lucien wanted Marianne to see her killer as the bird swooped down towards her, its beak twitching hungrily for the kill. Lying flat on her back, the bounty hunter began to laugh, a full-throated chuckle that burned her lungs.

"My dear brother," she murmured. "What a family we are."

And with that, she fished out the remote control from her shirt, the one connected to the battery of explosives she had planted along the east wall on her arrival. Marianne waited until the bird was almost upon her, and then pressed the button. There was a deep rumbling sound, a bright flash of light, and her world was engulfed in bricks and dust.

28

Jonathan was only a hundred yards away when the charges went off. There was a deep rumble like an earthquake, and the east wall gave a mighty shudder. For one second, and then another, nothing happened, and it looked as if the building had managed to withstand the blow. But then bricks came tumbling down like a waterfall, and the entire eastern wall of the power station collapsed as swiftly and decisively as a curtain on a stage.

The noise was deafening – the ground trembled underfoot. Jonathan hit the deck, covering his head with his hands.

"What the hell was that?" Carmichael screamed. The detective had been supervising the capture of the intruder when the explosion went off. Frustrated by the order to take him alive, the Darkside guards were roughly manhandling their hostage, muttering darkly about shooting him.

As the wall came down with a thunderous crash, Wilson watched with his mouth agape.

"Take the prisoner and bring the cars round!" Carmichael bellowed. "We need to get out of here. Come on, Charlie!"

The hunchback grabbed the stunned sergeant and ushered him back towards the power station, which now had only three sides to it. Clouds of dust were rising from the remnants of the east wall. On the west wall, Wilson saw the broad figure of Holborn hurry down the ladder towards them.

"I don't believe it!" he shouted. "The wall just came down!"

"So I saw," Carmichael said curtly. "Where's Lucien?"

"I couldn't see," Holborn replied. "There was too much dust." The Abettor surveyed the scene of destruction in front of them. "You don't think . . . that they're *both* gone?"

"I hate to disappoint you," a low voice called out from amongst the rubble, "but I'm still very much here."

Lucien Ripper hauled himself painfully down to the ground, his clothes in tatters and covered in dust. His cropped hair was nearly as white as Holborn's. The Black Phoenix had retreated back within him, leaving only a lame, bleeding human in its wake – a mere afterthought compared to the vile, powerful creature. Lucien coughed violently, flecks of blood daubing his lips.

"What on Darkside happened?" Holborn shouted.

"The wench had explosives," Lucien snarled, shaking off the Abettor's attempts to support him. "She blew up the entire wall. I only just managed to pull out in time. Why didn't your men start firing?"

"It seemed you had the situation under control, my

liege," Holborn said smoothly. "We thought our intervention was unnecessary."

"Have them rake through the rubble and make sure she's dead," Lucien ordered.

"Make sure?" Carmichael said incredulously, surveying the vast burial mound. "No one could have survived that."

"We have to be certain," Lucien said hoarsely.

"Actually, we have to get out of here," the hunchback contended. "There'll be police all over the place before you know it."

"I thought you had promised we wouldn't be disturbed tonight," Holborn said, his eyes narrowing.

"I said we were doing a training exercise, not that we were going to demolish the bloody building!" Carmichael yelled. "Do you have any idea how difficult it's going to be to explain this? We have to go – now!"

Lucien looked as though he was about to argue, but he was forestalled by another wracking coughing fit.

"You won," Carmichael continued, in a softer voice. "You are the new Ripper. Return to Darkside and prepare for your coronation." The detective smiled slyly. "Whilst you were fighting Marianne, our men captured an old friend of yours who will no doubt be delighted to take part in the celebrations."

"An old friend?" Lucien said quizzically.

A convoy of sleek cars was bumping across the wasteland, Darksiders leaning out of the windows to whoop and fire rounds into the air. As the lead car pulled up alongside them, Carmichael went round to the boot and popped it open. There, Lucien saw, tangled up in a heavy net, the unconscious form of Elias Carnegie.

"Well, well." A smile dawned on the Ripper's face. "It seems we have two reasons to celebrate."

Hiding behind a rock, Jonathan watched as Lucien climbed into the car and the cortege pulled away across the wasteland. He was nearly crying with frustration. Every sinew in his body yearned to run over and try to free his ally, but he knew it would be futile. As the cars slipped out through the exit and into the night, Jonathan clambered wearily to his feet. He had failed. Lucien had won the Succession, Marianne was dead, and Carnegie's sacrifice had meant nothing. He kicked out bitterly at a stone, sending it rattling loudly across the ground.

"Jonathan?" a voice called out. "Is that you?"

He whirled round, startled, only to see Raquella and Harry racing towards him from out of the gloom. His heart leapt.

"What are you doing here?" he asked, amazed.

"Looking for you," answered the maid. "We gambled that you wouldn't be far away from the fighting."

"But how did you know the Succession was taking place here?"

"Same way I find out every secret in Darkside," Harry said wryly. "Went to the *Informer* and asked Arthur Blake. It turned out that one of his contacts in Blackchapel has a big mouth on him. We got here as quickly as we could."

"I wish you'd got here sooner," Jonathan replied, his happiness fading. "Lucien and Holborn won the Succession. And they got Carnegie."

Raquella gasped. "Is he. . .?"

Jonathan shook his head. "They took him away in a car. I don't know what they're going to do to him." He paused. "Even though we'd argued, he came after me . . . sacrificed himself so I could . . . and then Marianne. . ."

He turned and looked at the remains of the power station.

"Jonathan?" Raquella said quietly.

There had to be thousands of bricks piled up there – tons of weight that had fallen directly on top of the bounty hunter. And yet Lucien had wanted to check. He had wanted to make sure Marianne was dead. It seemed a tiny chance, the slightest sliver of hope, but at that moment it was all Jonathan had.

He broke into a sprint and raced inside the power station, with Harry and Raquella hot on his heels. They watched as he clambered on top of the pile and began hurling bricks to one side.

"I know you want Marianne to be alive," the maid said hesitantly, "but there's no way. . ."

"Either help me or shut up!" Jonathan shouted, scrabbling frantically.

It was Harry who stepped forward, hauling heavy pieces of masonry out of the way to allow Jonathan to get to the heart of the rubble. The two boys got down and began to dig with their hands, and then Raquella was on her knees beside them, picking up bricks and throwing them to one side. They didn't speak, focusing all their energies on getting deeper and deeper into the debris. After minutes of digging in the darkness, their fingers sore and their faces caked in dust, Jonathan heaved a large stone to one side, and saw a flash of pale skin.

"She's here!" he called out.

He redoubled his efforts, the weariness evaporating from his muscles. It wasn't long before the three of them had cleared a space around the bounty hunter, and could look down upon her.

It was not a pretty sight. Marianne was as white as a corpse, her face streaked with dirt and blood and her left arm jutting out at an unnatural angle. She didn't appear to be breathing. Jonathan lifted her up as though she were made of bone china and carried her away from the rubble to a flat piece of ground, where he laid her down and pressed an ear against her chest.

And heard the faint, distant sound of a heartbeat.

"She's alive," he said.

"But that's impossible!" Raquella gasped.

"She's a Ripper," Harry replied. "It's not impossible at all."

"We have to get her to a hospital," Jonathan said.

"Here," Harry said, looping his arms beneath the bounty hunter's body. "Let me. You've done enough tonight."

Jonathan reluctantly moved out of the way, allowing

Harry to pick up his aunt in his strong arms. As the first police siren began wailing in the distance, a blue light breaking out of the darkness, they hurried away. They were close to the exit when Raquella stopped and grabbed Jonathan's arm.

"Wait," she said. "There's something I have to tell you. It can't wait." Looking at the maid now, Jonathan saw that her cheeks were streaked with tears. She pushed a crumpled sheet of parchment into his hands.

"What's this?" he said.

"We found it in La Mort's safety deposit box. I'm so sorry. . ."

Her voice trailed off as Jonathan began reading, his eyes straining to make out the words in the gloom. The parchment seemed to be some sort of official form, written in tight, spidery handwriting:

> *I, Dr Hugo La Mort, hereby attest that in my medical opinion the patient below suffers from a malady of the brain so acute that it is beyond the realm of medical treatment, and that the only remaining course of treatment is confinement to the Bedlam for a period of indeterminate incarceration.*

"I don't understand," Jonathan said.

"Look at the patient's name," Raquella said softly. And then he saw it, in crabbed handwriting at the bottom of the parchment: Theresa Starling.

"What's the Bedlam?" Jonathan asked numbly.

"It's a mental asylum in Darkside," Raquella replied. "La Mort's been sending people there for years – regardless of whether or not they were insane. I guess that Lucien must have paid him to commit your mum. I'm truly sorry."

"But then . . . this means he didn't kill her!" he said, his voice rising with excitement. "She could still be alive!"

"The Bedlam isn't like other asylums, Jonathan," Raquella said gently. "It is a dark, terrible place. This order was given over a decade ago. Even if she is still alive, you wouldn't want to see her now. The Bedlam changes people. This was a death sentence in all but name."

"We'll see about that," Jonathan replied stubbornly. "If Marianne can survive the Succession, my mum can survive this place."

"I know you'll want to go back," said Harry. "But you've got to understand: Lucien's ruling Darkside now. If we even set foot in there, he'll have us killed. And we haven't got Carnegie to help us out any more. What do you want us to do?"

"What do I want us to do?" Jonathan echoed. "It seems pretty simple to me. We get Marianne well again, rescue Carnegie, find my mum, and then go and kill Lucien."

Despite the starkness of his words, Jonathan felt a strange sense of calm wash over him. Even as bleak as things looked, he knew what he had to do.

"Are you with me?" he asked.

Harry laughed darkly, shifting Marianne's weight in his

arms. "Single-handedly storm Darkside? I wouldn't miss it for the world. I'm in."

"Raquella?"

The maid bit her lip, then nodded quickly.

"Good. Let's get out of here, then. We've got a lot of work to do."

With the air swelling with the sound of sirens, Jonathan turned his back on the shattered remnants of the power station, and led his friends deep into the London night.

to discover more?

Look out for the thrilling conclusion
to the Darkside saga, Blackjack –
coming soon.

And catch up on all the Darkside adventures,
now with a terrifying new look.

www.welcometodarkside.co.uk

Jonathan's home has been attacked. His dad's in an asylum.
He's running for his life. And there's nowhere to hide.

He's stumbled on the city's greatest secret:
Darkside.

A brutal killer is on the loose!

When Jonathan and Carnegie agree to investigate a series of vicious murders in Darkside, they don't realize what they've stumbled into. Jonathan soon discovers his mother was investigating a similar crime on the day she disappeared, and the trail starts to lead uncomfortably close to home.

Before long he finds himself embroiled in the borough's most dangerous secret – and its most dangerous family.